Teng Zhenfu

I0526961

Hunting the Lynx

Prunus Press USA

Original Title: 《猎猞》

This edition is published by arrangement with Prunus Press USA, through the agency of China National Publications Import and Export (Group) Co., Ltd.

HUNTING THE LYNX

Written by Teng Zhenfu

Translated by Haiwang Yuan

Designed by Brandy Ding

First edition 2022

ISBN: 978-1-61612-142-6

Prunus Press USA

ABOUT THE AUTHOR

Lao Teng, originally named Teng Zhenfu, was born in 1963. He is a Chinese writer, and a member of the China Writers Association. His publications include *Lietou Posthouse* (《腊头驿》), *Applause* (《鼓掌》), *Resorting to Force* (《刀兵过》), *Warring-States Red* (《战国红》), *Cherry Blossom Tour* (《樱花之旅》), *Training the Goshawk* (《熬鹰》), *A City without Ravens* (《没有乌鸦的城市》), and *Meeting Martyrs* (《会殇》). His other writings are represented by his essay collection *Notes on Confucianism* (《儒学笔记》).

NOTE ON THE TITLE

On the No. 3 Forest Farm of the Hinggan Mountains, hunters can say "kill" when catching tigers, bears, wolves, or boars. But, in the case of lynxes, they still stick to the more formal term "hunt."

1

Gold Tiger knew that Director Hu had set a trap to catch him. If he had fallen victim, the director's big dream of becoming a hunter terminator in No.3 Forest Farm would have come true. Upon arriving at the public security police station in the farm in the capacity of its head, Director Hu had promised to end hunting within its domain. In it, nine out of ten men had traditionally been intrepid hunters and good at using hunting weapons. Many were descendants of posthouse employees, and hunting had been their lifelong calling. After Director Hu took his position, the public security police office posted bulletins on confiscating hunting rifles everywhere, threatening to end the hunters' good days. After the bulletins were published, the cable TV of the forest farm also promoted the confiscation campaign. And the slogan sounded biting: "Refuse to hand in your rifle today, and you'll find your hands cuffed tomorrow!" Everyone knew what it meant and hated to waste a good part of their lives in jail.

Gold Tiger, however, adopted a wait-and-see attitude. He didn't care about what other hunters thought. He only focused on the five best-known ones. They had promised to him that they would never look at the bulletins. They said to him, "Hey, Sharpshooter, we'll follow your example. We won't hand in our rifles if you refuse to give up yours. We don't believe Director Hu will lock us all in a small cell!" But less than a week later, Buckteeth Liu surrendered his blunderbuss, followed by Third Brother Song and Li Ku. The two younger hunters gave their weapons up to the county public security bureau as they believed that the bureau would trade their shotguns with big prizes. Not only did they receive no award, but they also wasted their money on traveling expenses. The five hunters had been courteous enough to call Gold Tiger separately before their betrayal. Their excuse was about the same: "Bro, we have no alternative but to give in. Director Hu calls me once a day and gets more threatening each time. He's simply driving me crazy!" Gold Tiger thought of the police station head as funny: He called every one of the five except him. He suspected he was intentional: He laid a trap for him.

"I'll never let Director Hu have his way," thought Gold Tiger, "I'll hand in the Red Arrow since I've got to. I won't give the director a handle against myself."

What he said about the Red Arrow was not an arrow. It was a small-caliber hunting rifle modeled on the Russian TOZ-8 type. A brand-name product of the Qinghua Factory in Bei'an, it boasted excellent accuracy of fire. Therefore, Red Arrow was Gold Tiger's apple of the eye. He was reluctant because he found it too hard to tear himself from it. "Without Red Arrow, am I still a Gold Tiger?" He felt losing his confidence in himself.

Gold Tiger called his rifle Red Arrow because an oxide layer appeared on its pear-wood stock due to long-term use, and the grains looked as dark red as a bloodstain. The stock also looked like a rusted arrowhead, so he gave the rifle its name, signifying a bloodstained arrow.

After the No. 3 Forest Farm Police Station put up the bulletin, Gold Tiger held off, giving up his rifle. He was rubbing his Red Arrow again and again with a piece of deerskin. Hunters felt obligated to clean their hunting rifles every day, whether using them or not. While rubbing them, the hunters had to talk to them, telling them what they were doing. Some hunters would seal their weapons with butter. That was not Gold Tiger's style. How could he befriend it if he had left it in the cold? *Only when you care for your rifle can it live up to your expectations! Cleaning it immediately before using it is like making friends with someone you want to ask for help at once. That's nothing but a one-time deal.*

The public security police officers knew who had hunting rifles and what brands they were in its jurisdiction. After publicizing their notification, none of the hunters dared to hide their weapons. Each stepped out of the police station teary-eyed after leaving them behind. Golden Arrow saw Miao Kui give up his newly bought shotgun obediently. He had never used it. It seemed as if he had bought it just to deliver it up. But he knew the secret behind Miao Kui's behavior.

Gold Tiger was aware that Director Hu had his eyes on him. *I own it because I'm called Sharpshooter!* This nickname made him the obvious target. *The nail that sticks up mostly gets hammered down. Who else would Director focus on if not me?* Director Hu had an angular face, bleached hair and whiskers, and light-brown eyes. He would be a nightmare to anyone who got his attention with such a look.

Since Director Hu had a grudge with him, Gold Tiger contemplated that he would probably use the rifle-confiscating campaign as an excuse to hurt him. Brother the Sixth, a hunter-turned auxiliary policeman in the station, was Gold Tiger's diehard follower. He confided to Gold Tiger that Director Hu talked tough, saying, "Sharpshooter the is the ringleader of the hunters, right? Let's wait and see!" Brother the Sixth said he would mean it when he spoke with the pet phrase, thinking he would be bound to win.

On the deadline day, an hour before off duty, all the seven police officers had put on their guns, their eyes ping-ponging from their watches to Director Hu's face. They were so tense that they seemed like an arrow ready to go from the bow. Director Hu had given the order: as soon as the clock struck five, they would go and "summon" Gold Tiger. In fact, they meant to take him to the police station by force, not to invite him like a guest.

The second hand on the quartz clock that had worked quietly before now raced, ticking and ticking. It seemed to jitter on the police officers' nerves, with each blood vein becoming a sensor. They couldn't help being nervous. It was because the Sharpshooter they were going to "summon" was such a marksman that he wouldn't miss any target at which he aimed. The bullet would never veer to a target's forehead if he wanted to shoot at his nose bridge. If he gained vantage ground, he could wipe out the seven police officers with his small-caliber rifle hands down. Therefore, this operation was as good as catching a serial killer.

Director Hu was composed. Sitting at the desk, he was cracking pine nuts to enjoy the kernels, and cracking nuts in the mouth required strong teeth. He picked up one and tossed it into his mouth. The "crack" sound gave the others a shudder. Then, he spat out the broken shell and ground the kernel in his mouth with relish. Cracking pine nuts and making it sound like igniting firecrackers before a life-and-death confrontation gave the people around him goosebumps.

The gate of the police station faced the west on the street. It was open, with the setting sun shining on its whitish cement ground, as shiny as a giant TV screen. It was a quarter past four. A long shadow extended into it slowly, making the screen larger and larger until it occupied the entire yard. It was Gold Tiger. Not only did he have his rifle slung over his shoulder, but he also carried a black plastic bag in one hand. His bumpy face was gloomy but unclear, with his back to the sun. His disheveled hair, however, appeared eye-catching. Placing the rifle and the plastic bag on the desk, he took out two unsealed boxes filled with bullets from the pack. Then, he said to the police officers, "Everything's here."

Director Hu rose and studied Gold Tiger's face with vigilance. Then, he picked up the rifle and pulled back the bolt expertly, saying, "A good one! And it's clean!" After that, he handed it to a police officer by his side.

"Can we go through some procedures?" asked Gold Tiger.

The auxiliary police officer named Brother the Sixth passed him a form and asked him to fill in the type of the rifle and put his thumbprint on it.

"Done, right?" Gold Tiger asked again.

"Of course, it's done since you've surrendered your rifle." Director Hu sat down and then said to the others with a relaxed tone, "It's five. You're ready to get off." Gold Tiger could positively discern Director Hu's frustration, thinking that his deliberate effort to set the trap failed, and his idea of wait and see came to nothing. *I would be surprised if he didn't appear so disappointed.*

Director Hu and Gold Tiger bearing each other grudges were known to everyone in No. 3 Forest Farm. Their enmity originated from three incidents. One was a shooting contest. Coming on top as a crack shot had been a way to acquire the chieftaincy of a bandit gang in the past. It was an actual match between the best sharpshooters. The bandits set a wine bowl on top of a gang member, and the bullet would hit the bowl holder's head if a shooter missed his target. Upon assu-ming his position in No. 3 Forest Farm, Director Hu learned about Gold Tiger's nickname "Sharpshooter." He yearned to see if he could beat him in marksmanship. The director had been transferred from the army, where he had been his division's famed sharpshooter. Therefore, he had looked down upon Gold Tiger, an amateur shooter. They competed in three events: shooting a fixed and then a moving target with a rifle and shooting at a target 30 meters away with a handgun. Gold Tiger won the two rifle events, while Director Hu won only the handgun match. Another incident had to do with recruiting an auxiliary police officer. Director Hu found a talent in Gold Tiger and sent someone to talk with him. Gold Tiger asked if an auxiliary police officer wore a police uniform. When he was told that he would be given a security guard uniform without a police emblem attached to it, Gold Tiger wrote the job off. He said something to irritate Director Hu, "Working with someone I've defeated? No way!" No one had embarrassed Director Hu like him in No. 3 Forest Farm. Gold Tiger could have rejected his offer, but he shouldn't have said something to hurt him. Then, someone heard the director say that Gold Tiger was pretending that he was important and that he would let him wait and see! The third incident involved saw Gold Tiger being fined. It was the most shameful moment in his life. It started with him catching a boar by setting a trap on the mountain. The police caught and fined him and locked him overnight in a small dark room. Brother the Sixth told him in secret, "You're lucky, Brother Gold! They would have confiscated your Red Arrow if you had brought it." Gold Tiger thought it was a good fortune not to have taken the rifle with him that day. In fact, after the new hunting regulations were introduced, he did everything he could to avoid using the firearm when hunting. He believed he was detained because Director Hu deliberately found fault with him. The wild boars in the mountain were worth nothing. Only he was locked up while other hunters who had done the same were spared any punishment.

Loathing to see Director Hu's light-brown eyes, Gold Tiger said goodbye and turned to leave. But Director Hu suddenly asked, "What can you do without your rifle?"

Gold Tiger responded to Director Hu behind him without turning his head, "I'll take care of Miao Kui's sheep."

"So, do you think a shepherd is more dignified than an auxiliary police officer?" Director Hu's tone was obviously satirical. Even if Gold Tiger had wanted to work as one now, Director Hu wouldn't have allowed him. His question was retaliator, trying to embarrass Gold Tiger.

"Miao Kui is my brother," said Gold Tiger as he turned around.

"A famous Sharpshooter now turns into a shepherd. It doesn't sound right to me," said Director Hu as he went up to a washbasin, twisted a towel, and wiped his hand. Gold Tiger saw Director Hu making a great effort as if he were wrenching the towel apart. Suddenly, a Chinese proverb sneaked into Gold Tiger's mind: he was "washing his hands in a gold basin." Unlike the English idiom "wash one's hands of," it has the connotation of "giving up doing something while one is on top." Gold Tiger hoped that Director Hu would be satisfied enough not to hurt him anymore.

"I heard that you're good at shooting 'flying dragons,' eh?" Director Hu dried his hands, balled the towel, and tossed it back to the washbasin. The "flying dragon" is a popular name for a bird known as hazel grouse.

A descendent of an ancient posthouse employee, Gold Tiger, carried on the unique skill of shooting "flying dragons" from his ancestors. He had quite a few fans among the hunters because he only aimed at the head of the bird and rarely missed it. It makes sense to shoot the head because if the bullet enters the body, its lead poison will circulate to change the meat flavor. Then, chefs would find it hard to concoct a soup out of it. The "flying dragon" is one of the eight sources of the most delicious fowl meat. Matchlessly savory, the "flying-dragon" soup is a delicacy known far and wide.

"I washed my hands in a gold basin long ago. Now that 'flying dragons' are on the national list of protected species, I don't want to break the law."

Caught off-guard, Director Hu chuckled, "It's odd that a Sharpshooter becomes environmentally aware!"

Feeling that the conversation was getting disagreeable, Gold Tiger turned around and stormed out of the police station.

Director Hu didn't stop teasing him behind him, "Don't hunt rabbits while herding your sheep."

Gold Tiger retorted, "No one can stop me if I want to."

Standing there with his arms akimbo, Director Hu tilted his head to the side, watching Gold Tiger walking into the distance. Then, he said to his subordinates filling the room, "We'll wait and see!"

Later, Brother the Sixth told Director Hu that Gold Tiger could hunt without a rifle. He was not only a marksman but an expert in setting snares, and he seldom missed his prey. He had gotten a bear three decades before. It was rare to snare a bear in the history of the forest farm. Although this ancient method of trapping animals had been used until now, only animals prone to startles, such as Siberian roe deer, true deer, and wild boars, would fall victim. Bears were mighty. They would struggle out of or bite off the snaring device unless it incapacitated them. Upon hearing Gold Tiger's resourcefulness, Director Hu rolled his light-brown eyes and said to Brother the Sixth, "Wasn't Monkey King omnipotent? But he couldn't escape the Buddha's hand, could he?" [1]

After surrendering his rifle, Gold Tiger worked as a shepherd, known in northern Chinese vernacular as *yangguanr*. It's a compound word formed of two characters: *yang* (sheep or goat) and *guanr*, pronounced the same as *guan* (official). Therefore, *yangguanr* sounds like "an official overseeing a flock of sheep." Gold Tiger felt content, congratulating himself deprecatingly on becoming an official in his fifties. He remembered watching a TV show that asked viewers to guess riddles. One of them was "Picking an official from a thousand people," with the answer being "guanr." [2] Working as a shepherd, he

---

[1] This reference is from *Journey to the West*, one of the four classic Chinese novels. It depicts a monk from Tang China seeking genuine Buddhist sutras from India, escorted by three demigod disciples. One of them is Monkey King, who can travel thousands of miles with a single somersault and change himself into 72 forms. When he revolted against the Jade Emperor of Heaven, the latter called in the Buddha to subdue him. Seeing Monkey King bragging about his prowess, the Buddha challenged him to escape from his hand. Of course, the holy hand can extend wherever the monkey goes. Eventually, the Buddha suppressed him with the Five-finger Mountain until the Tang monk came to get him out to become his escorting disciple.

[2] The Chinese character for *guanr* is 倌. It's composed of the radical 亻 (person) and the root character 官 (official, pronounced as *guan*). It means a minor "official or officer." The radical 亻 becomes 千 (meaning "thousand") with a 一 (meaning "one") crossing its vertical stroke. The Chinese 挑 is a polysemy, meaning both "select" and "take away by picking." Therefore, the riddle "Pick one (official) out of a thousand" is a pun: taking the one (一) away from the thousand (千). The result is 亻 with the root word 官 (official). Therefore, the answer to the riddle is 倌 (*guanr*).

had plenty of spare time. So, Gold Tiger wanted a dog as his companion. He loved Tibetan mastiffs. One of them would be as good as three wolves. The mastiff is the only dog breed that isn't afraid of wild animals. He shared his thought with Miao Kui, who gave him full support and arranged for a cart to take him to North Town, Liaoning Province. It was known as the largest dog market in the country. He chose carefully and finally bought one belonging to the Red Tibetan Mastiff breed. It was a large-size, one-year-old male with perfect hair color. With had lion-like paws and triangular eyes above prominent lacrimal sacs, it looked like the king of the beasts. Gold Tiger could tell intuitively that this red Tibetan mastiff would indeed become the cream of the crop with proper training. The Red Mastiff made up for Gold Tiger's loss of his Red Arrow. He and Red Mastiff were almost inseparable. To protect the young mastiff from sudden attacks from other dogs, Gold Tiger bought a stainless-steel collar with double-row spikes. He would put it on the mastiff when unchaining it.

The day Gold Tiger bought Red Mastiff, Miao Kui's wife gave birth to her third son. She was overage for childbirth. The smooth delivery came as a blessing for the Miao family. Miao Kui had no alternative but to have this third child. Gold Tiger witnessed the Miao family's misery as a neighbor: they lost their eldest son at a tender age, and their second son was born with a hearing disorder. So, this newborn became the family's only hope. To keep this son safe from diseases and disasters, superstitious Miao Kui invited an able fortuneteller to give the newborn a name. The fortuneteller said that a child with a humble name would be easier to rear. Therefore, he suggested naming the child Gousheng, literally meaning "Dog's Leftover." But Gold Tiger's wife objected adamantly that time had changed and that he would be ridiculed at school when he grew up. Thinking that since his son was born on the day he brought the mastiff home, Miao Kui said, "Let's call him Ji'ao. Ao is pronounced the same as a mastiff and sounds better than dog's leftover." [3]

Miao Kui had a faint heart. Even a rabbit darting out of a clump of grass would startle him. At night, he didn't dare to walk from home to the company, a distance of only a mile or so. Each time, he would ask Gold Tiger to keep him company. An epicure, Miao Kui saw thought of the flavor of the meat whenever he saw an animal of a fowl. He was a good judge of mountain delicacies and could tell a lot about them. For example, he said that a pheasant's meat was too harsh, a wild boar's too fatty, a Siberian roe deer's too dry, and a rabbit's too plain. He stated that, the best delicacies included moose noses, bear paws, and "flying dragons," which he wouldn't trade for shark fins. Gold Tiger was different from Miao Kui in that he might be a first-class shooter, but he wasn't fond of eating wild animals and fowls. Without an appetite for them, he enjoyed the sense of conquest when hunting them. He felt uncomfortable when he saw some hunters slitting open the belly

---

[3] Though written differently, mastiff and the sizeable marine turtle in Chinese mythology share the same pronunciation, "ao." Associated with the legendary Chinese creator Nüwa, the turtle Ao is one of the Chinese Dragon's nine sons. One who can stand on the head of Ao is supposed to be the cream of the crop. Therefore, Ji'ao (Lucky Turtle) is a name that may not sound pretty but carries the father's good wish and hope.

of a roe deer, gutting it, and eating its liver raw before cooking its meat in a pot hanging above a makeshift fire pit. To him, the behavior was comparable to killing POWs. Miao Kui had bought two Austrian-made shotguns of the same brand. He stowed them at home to exorcize evil spirits from the house. After the bulletins about surrendering guns were posted, Miao Kui handed in one of them while hiding the other at home. He could fool anyone else but Gold Tiger because Miao Kui had told him about his purchase of the two brand-name shotguns and even flaunted them to him several times. Gold Tiger could tell he had a pair judging from the quality of the wood stocks: one was walnut and the other maple, which he could tell very well. But Gold Tiger kept the secret to himself, thinking that Miao Kui had bought the guns only to give himself courage. He wouldn't have to get scared by chanced break-ins if he had the guns at home.

Miao Kui never hunted with the guns he bought. He told Gold Tiger to ask if he wanted to borrow it, saying, "You may treat it as yours. The only thing I'd like to ask back is a morsel of the meat from your game." "Why did you buy a gun in the first place since you don't hunt?" Miao Kui responded, "Let me tell you why. A wushu master never uses his sword in a hand-to-hand fight, but he always has a sword at his waist. That's why I bought the gun." Gold Tiger thought that he had read too many swordsman fictions because wushu masters not using their weapons was nonexistent in real life. However, he felt that Miao Kui did the right thing not to use his. Not many people who used rifles or shotguns knew that weapons never boded well, and accidents would aptly happen to nonexperts. A hunter in No. 3 Forest Farm had accidentally shot his wife through and through while rubbing his rifle. Miao Kui said he never loaded his gun. He had locked the bullets in a safe. They wouldn't become rogue bullets even if they had so desired.

Miao Kui considered it a shame for Gold Tiger to have "washed his hands in a gold basin." He asked, "You're afraid of Director Hu, aren't you?"

Gold Tiger shook his head and responded, "I was a few years ago. But there's a reason for what I did this time."

"Why couldn't you ignore it?" asked Miao Kui.

"Well, my granddaughter gave me the idea," said Gold Tiger. "One day, I went hunting in the mountain and got a roe deer and a few rabbits. My daughter came to visit me that day, bringing my granddaughter, who was only two then. Seeing the game, she cried. My daughter asked her why. She said her grandpa was a bad guy, even worse than the big gray wolf. He killed the cutie deer and bunnies. My granddaughter mistook the roe deer for the common deer. But her words kept me awake overnight, thinking of how much animal blood I had on my hands."

With his eyes wide open, Miao Kui said, "So, the way you said it, I shouldn't eat hunted meat, either."

Gold Tiger raised his head and looked into the distant mountains, saying, "You'd better not. We'll have peace of mind if we stop sinning."

"You're trying to be a Buddhist," said Miao Kui, who felt the Gold Tiger had changed into a different person.

"Another incident gave me the revelation," Gold Tiger began to relate a hunting experience of his. *That day, I shot a wolf in the Cork Tree Gully. I got its belly. Usually, it couldn't run anymore. But he did, howling. I traced the bloodstain to the edge of an earth tableland. I found the wolf beneath it, the front part in a cave. It was motionless. I guessed it was dead and dragged it out by the tail, only to find a litter of pups. They gazed at me in panic.* Gold Tiger continued, "My heart melted right there. The dying wolf was trying to protect its babies by stopping up the cave opening with its body. It was motherhood that defied death! I turned and left the den quickly, hoping that the male wolf was still alive so the pups wouldn't be starved to death. At the moment of my turning away, I felt proud of myself. Who says that hunters are cold killers? I am not, at least!"

Miao Kui said, "Female wolves are the most protective of their pups."

Gold Tiger nodded, saying, "I had had nightmares for three nights running. I regretted destroying the entire litter."

"What did you dream about?"

"I dreamt of a litter of wolf pups crowding around me asking me to give their mother back. They fixed their eyes at me pathetically. From that day on, dog puppies I saw would always remind me of the pups. It's hard to tell wolf pups from dog puppies at their nursing stage."

Miao Kui thought that the famed Sharpshooter in No. 3 Forest Farm had changed. His change was not due to the loss of his rifle. Neither was it because of Director Hu.

2

Gold Tiger drove the sheep into the mountain to graze not because he wanted to save fodder but because sheep raised in free range would yield better-quality meat.

Miao Kui's baby son always cried at night. Annoyed, he would often go with Gold Tiger to relieve himself in the mountain.

The mountains in the Hinggan range are mostly gently sloped, mostly covered with trees and grass. They constitute ideal grazing land. Miao Kui drove the flock into the grassland, where Red Mastiff became a shepherd. Gold Tiger lay down on the gravels in an opening to bask in the sunshine. The sky was bright blue, with fluffy clouds lingering there, appearing like cotton candy, a favorite in his childhood.

Miao Kui came over and lay down beside him with a tender grass blade beneath his teeth. It was from the Physalis alkekengi plant, popularly known as *suanjiang* (literally "sour berry") in Chinese and Chinese lantern in English. Children all liked to eat it. Looking at the sky, Miao Kui asked, "Can you tell what wild animal is the most ferocious?"

"There's a popular saying, 'A boar is as good as two bears and three tigers,'" responded Gold Tiger. "It's not without reasons. I've never run into a tiger, but I came into grips with boars and bears. Bears are reckless, whereas boars are violent. It's easy to dodge a reckless bear, but fighting a savage boar, specifically a lone boar, is challenging. It chases anyone it sees and bites the one it can reach. Wild boars have hurt many hunters."

"No wonder wild boars are rated ahead of the other animals," gasped Miao Kui.

"A man who is horny fears no law; a boar in heat fears no death. So, a male boar in heat is a terrifying animal. Hormones work the best in wild boars and can double their fighting capacity. Except for the sows, everyone is their sworn enemy in their eyes. Gold Tiger paused and went on, "But what we said is not entirely correct. I think the lynx is the hardest to deal with among the animals in the mountains. It's a big cat with a tuft of hair on the tips of its ears."

"I've heard of lynxes but never seen one."

"A lynx is not very big, but its bite is fatal. Zhang San is fierce, right? But it cuts and runs as soon as it lays its eyes on a lynx."

Zhang San was the nickname of a wolf. How could people not be afraid of an animal that scared even a wolf? Miao Kui shuddered.

The sheep grazed leisurely in the open meadow. Suddenly, the flock became a little restless. Red Mastiff barked, "Woof, woof, woof!" It sounded like a boombox with considerable penetrating power. Gold Tiger was surprised. *Why is Red Mastiff reacting so abnormally since there're no beasts of prey in this area?* He sat up and saw Red Mastiff barking toward the direction behind the graveled opening. *Something must be happening there.* He called Red Mastiff over and leased it. Then, he had the dog lead him to the place behind the opening. He had walked around when he caught sight of a fox coiling in the thicket of grass. It was female and appeared silvery gray except for its eye sockets, muzzle, and paws, which were all white. One of the poor animal's front paws was caught in a foothold trap. Sticking up its ears and baring its teeth, the fox stared at the strangers in panic. Gold Tiger pulled Red Mastiff back. Once he let go of the leash, the giant mastiff would have torn the slim fox into pieces. Miao Kui rushed over and took out his smartphone to take a photo of the fox with his trembling hand. It was the first time he saw a trapped animal, and it was none other than a fox. The fox drew itself back hard, trying to break away as it snarled. The hunter's foothold trap was like a handcuff: the tighter it got, the more violently the cuffed person would struggle. If it had caught the silvery gray fox by its neck, it would have strangled it to death long before. Luckily, it captured only its paw and spared its life.

With Gold Tiger and Red Mastiff by his side, Miao Kui was slightly emboldened. He sized up the fox and said, "Its fur is good scarf material."

Gold Tiger shook his head, saying, "Descendants of posthouses have never hunted foxes. It's an accident."

Miao Kui echoed, "Yes, I've never heard of anyone snaring a fox."

"It's only a passing fox. Its den isn't nearby."

"What shall we do?" asked Miao Kui.

"Set it free, of course," responded Gold Tiger without hesitance.

Miao Kui asked, "If I go over to free it from the trap, will it bite me?"

"Yes, it will." Freeing a living creature from a trap was a dangerous business. Gold Tiger had tried to set a trapped rabbit free and got bitten. That accident taught him to understand the truth of the time-honored proverb: "An angry rabbit can bite." [④] Gold Tiger tethered Red Mastiff to a tree and went into a grove. He came out with a branch and handed it to Miao Kui as he said, "As you pin the fox's head down, I'll cut off the trap." With that, Gold Tiger pulled a knife from his boot. Its blade was a little shorter than a regular dagger but extremely sharp. It was a self-defense weapon that the local hunters found indispensable. Miao Kui inched closer to the fox, trying to pinch its head down. But the animal backed at first, but when the rope on the trap was pulled tight like a bow drawn to the fullest, it suddenly pounced forward. With a "crack," it leaped by Miao Kui's shoulder and scampered away limping. It left its bloody paw in the trap. Red Mastiff also lunged simultaneously only to be pulled back by the chain. It struggled with it like a raging bull.

Miao Kui's hesitancy had given the fox the time to spring up in desperation.

"Good Heavens! I didn't expect that a fox could be so powerful!" Miao Kui's fear still lingered.

"It was some fox!" Sighed Gold Tiger, "It would break its paw to run for its life. It took death-defying courage."

On their way back, Miao Kui suddenly whispered, "It's odd. Why

---

[④] The Chinese believe that rabbits, the allegedly meekest animals, never bite. Hence, the proverb means a cornered enemy can be deadly dangerous.

did the fox cry like a baby?"

Gold Tiger didn't respond. Hunters of the posthouse employees had abided by an unwritten law: treating foxes as their friends. He had had no idea why their ancestors laid down this implicit law. Later, a *zhiqing* (a member of the urban youth willingly or unwillingly lived and worked in the rural areas during the Cultural Revolution) gave him a convincing explanation. The forest farms used to be vulnerable to hemorrhagic fever, a kind of plague in the past. If infected, nine out of ten would die. The virus's host was the rat, and foxes were expert rat catchers. Where there were many foxes, the number of infected people would drop. Therefore, their ancestors had every reason to ban hunting foxes. For that matter, the hunters seldom killed weasels and owls. They were also capable rat hunters. They were "beneficial" animals and birds to use a modern term.

Little Ji'ao worried Miao Kui a lot. Since his birth, he had had a poor appetite and constantly cried at night. Medical exams showed that all the vitals were normal. Miao Kui doubted that he might be suffering from a mysterious kind of hysteria. Therefore, he invited the fortuneteller back to see what was going on. The fortuneteller spent quite some time trying everything he could: calling back the spirit of the sick baby, drawing magic incantations, and burning paper effigies. But all his efforts were in vain. Gold Tiger said comfortingly, "All babies cry. I don't think Little Ji'ao is sick at all." But Miao Kui considered constantly crying at night abnormal. He wouldn't allow anything wrong to happen to Ji'ao.

The day after Miao Kui's encounter with the silvery gray fox, a friend texted him, telling him that a shaman in No. 4 Forest Farm with Lao Mo as his last name could treat all kinds of hysteria. He had contacted him and asked Miao Kui to come over and look. According to the friend, this shaman could work wonders. Many people had gone to see him, and group photos with celebrities hung all over the walls in his house.

Only a dirt road through a wilderness led to No. 4 Forest Farm. Miao Kui didn't have the guts even to drive there by himself. So, Gold Tiger went with him, bringing his Red Mastiff along. The off-road jeep bumped along the dirt road covered with Ziziphus jujuba bushes and mugworts. It took them a two-hour drive to get to No. 4 Forest Farm. With the help of passers-by, who showed them the direction, they eventually found their way to the Lao Mo family. Built on a high foundation with an A-frame roof, Lao Mo's house was as conspicuous in the farm's residential area as a crane standing among a flock of chickens. There was a long wooden table with mottled paint in the yard, surrounded by long benches. It seemed to be the consultation platform. Lao Mo was taking a nap. After his wife woke him up, he looked languid and reluctant. To Gold Tiger's surprise, Lao Mo's sluggishness vaporized when he saw Red Mastiff. He reached out to greet the dog, his brown eyes shining at Red Mastiff like a pair of focused spotlights. The otherwise fearless dog shunned Lao Mo's look. Gold Tiger could feel the gentle quiver through the chain in his hand. The phenomenon had never happened before. Gold Tiger glanced at

Lao Mo and found his eyes shooting out beams of cold light, which could make people tremble with fear.

"It's a good dog," said Lao Mo, "It can yield 10 kilograms of meat at the very least."

The remark made Gold Tiger seethe with anger. *How can you praise a dog like this?! Dogs are hunters' loyal companions. A shaman should love dogs. How can you think of eating it? Besides, shamans aren't allowed to do so. Not only shaman, but all the descendants of the posthouses, the Oroqen, Daur, and some other minority ethnic peoples don't eat dogs, either.*

Miao Kui explained why he came to see him and told him Ji'ao's birthday and bazi. [5] He then placed a package of baijiu (high-proof Chinese liquor) of the Beidacang brand on the table close to one of its corners. His friend had told him that Lao Mo was fond of high-proof alcohol. He had bought the baijiu of this brand as a present for their first-time meeting. Lao Mo sat down and signaled Miao Kui to be seated without heeding Gold Tiger's presence. Lao Mo closed his eyes and counted on his fingers before opening his eyes in no time. He lit a cigarette and puffed out a series of smoke rings. Then, he stubbed it out in an ashtray, looked up, and said, staring into Miao Kui's eyes, "Your son has a poor appetite, feels frightened, cries at night, passes loose stool, and loses weight, doesn't he?"

---

[5] *Bazi* (Four Pillars of Destiny) literally means "eight characters." It's a Chinese astrological concept that a person's fate can be foretold by examining the Stems-and-Branches assigned to his birth hour, day, month, and year.

Miao Kui nodded repeatedly. The five symptoms that Lao Mo described were all correct. Lao Mo continued, "Demons and ghosts also love an adorable child. But their affection doesn't bode well. So, we'd better drive them away." Lao Mo's words were scary because exorcizing the evil spirits was no ordinary people's job.

"Master, please do me a favor. You're our only hope to save my son." With that, Miao Kui took out a red envelope with cash and put it on the wooden table. *Money can work miracles. I have to lose some money to avert the misfortune.* He added, "I'll double our gratuity after my son recovers."

Lao Mo didn't touch the red envelope. Instead, he cast his eyes on the package of baijiu liquor. "I can certainly come up with a prescription. But some of the ingredients may be hard to come by."

"What is it? Miao Kui asked in all earnest.

"Go and hunt a lynx. Skin its head and make a hat with the ears intact for your son. Then, no demons or ghosts will bother him anymore."

Gold Tiger was taken aback: the lynx is a protected animal. Hunting it would result in imprisonment. He felt that this shaman's prescription was a sham: he gave Miao Kui a hard nut to crack as he knew lynx poaching wasn't allowed. It was an impossible mission, and Miao Kui could not blame his failure to get a lynx on him so that the myth of him working wonders would remain. Gold Tiger had previous contacts with quite a few wizards who gave various strange prescriptions with easily accessible herbs but hard-to-get efficacy-enhancers, such as tiger's urine, dragon's whiskers, or bladder stones of cows or hogs. They just intentionally made things difficult.

"Hunting a lynx? You mean hunting a lynx?" asked Miao Kui. It was the first time he had heard the term "hunting."

"He knows it. You can ask him for details after you get back," said Lao Mo, pointing at Gold Tiger. Perhaps, he had guessed that Gold Tiger was a hunter.

"It's extremely challenging to hunt lynxes," Gold Tiger cut in. "I've never huntd lynxes though I've been a hunter all my life."

"You're right. I've seen patients for over a dozen years, and I've never written out prescriptions with easy-to-get ingredients." Lao Mo's eyes showed some contempt.

Other visitors came and waited outside the courtyard. Miao Kui and Gold Tiger said goodbye and left. Miao Kui rolled down the window of his jeep and waved at Lao Mo. Suddenly, Red Mastiff, which had been quiet all the time, barked in its booming voice, which sounded like a lion's roar. Lao Mo, standing at the door, lost his continence abruptly. He turned quickly and withdrew.

"Why is catching lynxes called hunting them?" asked Miao Kui.

"Lynxes are cunning, fierce, and difficult to catch. Hunting shows contempt, like an adult beating a child. It's a cinch. When hunting an animal, you treat it as your equal, and you must be courageous and intelligent. So, it makes sense for the hunters in the forest farm to refer to catching lynxes as hunting them. People regard those who can hunt lynxes highly. I've hunted wild animals all my life, but I've never hunted a lynx."

"Does a lynx-fur hat work?" Miao Kui recalled Lao Mo's prescription.

Gold Tiger knew that the Oroqen people had a habit of having their women and children wearing lynx-fur hats. It seemed that Lao Mo also knew it. *The claim that such a hat can scare away demons and ghosts is unconvincing. Besides, who says that monsters and ghosts exist?* "No matter what, it doesn't hurt to wear one. But the problem is that hunting lynxes are against the law."

"Wizards' prescriptions are all very odd," said Miao Kui.

Gold Tiger chuckled, "They wouldn't be called wizards if their prescriptions were not weird."

Gold Tiger remembered Lao Mo's look when he stared at Red Mastiff. He asked Miao Kui to call his friend and learn why Lao Mo was interested in dogs. After the phone was connected, the friend said that Lao Mo was fond of dog meat. He bought a dozen or more dogs every year. He would then slaughter and eat them. "No matter how fierce a dog is," said he, "it would tremble when seeing him."

"I see!" Gold Tiger realized what had happened to Red Mastiff. He said, "Butchers have the scent of killing, which man can't detect. But dogs, cows, hogs, and sheep can smell it. That was what Red Mastiff did, and that was why he recoiled and tried to hide behind me all the time."

Miao Kui knitted his brows and said, "It's paradoxical for a butcher to be a shaman."

"Yes, something must be wrong. A shaman isn't supposed to eat dog meat," echoed Gold Tiger.

Miao Kui said, "Who else can we trust for this matter if we don't trust him? No one."

"But Lao Mo gave you a hard nut to crack." Gold Tiger was aware that this ball was in his court because Miao Kui would never hunt lynxes in the mountains.

"You know I don't even have the guts to kill a rabbit. How can I hunt a lynx?" said Miao Kui, awkwardly. "I'm just a foodie. I need your help this time."

"I've promised to Director Hu that I'll never hunt again. I can't break it."

Miao Kui said, "Please think again. Or you can help me make a lynx-hunting plan at the very least. You'll be my advisor, and that would be enough help."

Miao Kui's entreat amused Gold Tiger. He said to himself, "A lynx-foraging plan? You'd better call it a Marshal Plan."

The road was bumpy. The sand and gravels used to pave it were heaped like grave mounds, appearing pretty ominous. The off-road jeep jogged up and down. As they drove along, they talked about nothing but lynxes.

3

Gold Tiger saw Miao Kui fiddling with his shotgun in the house through the window.

Gold Tiger knew what Miao Kui was up to: he was getting ready to hunt lynxes. For some reason, Gold Tiger suddenly called to mind the dark cell in the police station. It was dimly lit by a low wattage bulb protected by an iron mesh hanging high from the ceiling. Mold covered all the walls, in which there was no window. A portable toilet made of an empty paint container diffused a stinking smell. A plank bed was covered with a straw mat instead of a mattress. It squeaked when he sat upon it. Locked up in it was like being confined in the nether world. It gave you're the creepy feeling of being haunted. Gold Tiger imagined that Miao Kui would be scared to death if he stayed in it for a few days.

One day, he and Miao Kui were chit-chatting in the latter's office when Director Hu invited himself into it.

"You're a rare guest!" Miao Kui stood up and greeted him. "It isn't easy for Director Hu to come and visit. Let's have some small talk." Gold Tiger nodded his greetings and started absent-mindedly browsing a newspaper he picked up from the coffee table.

Director Hu plopped himself down in the quilted couch, scanning back and forth with his light-brown eyes as if to look for something. Gold Tiger locked his stealthy gaze at Director Hu from the corners of his eyes, aware that he came with ill intent.

A goshawk specimen was behind the couch, its wings spreading as far as two meters. It was set on a root sculpture, assuming the posture of swooping down. Director Hu sat right in front of the specimen with his sharp light brown eyes, reminding Gold Tiger of the image of Vulture, the bandit chieftain he had seen in a 3D movie. Vulture's eyes also had the same color as Director Hu's.

"Nowadays, many wild animals are protected from hunting, don't you know, Gold Tiger?" Director Hu didn't address Miao Kui. Instead, he stared at Gold Tiger's face.

The question was not new to Gold Tiger. Bulletins were posted in the display case to disseminate information about protecting the forests from wildfires at the junction of the roads leading into the woods. "I've nothing to do with hunting anymore," responded Gold Tiger, "I'm a shepherd now."

"You're still a Sharpshooter," said Director Hu, sitting with one leg crossing the other and one foot in the air. "Hunting is like using drugs. It's easy to get addicted to but hard to give up."

Miao Kui asked, "Can we still hunt wild boars and wolves?"

"It's written black and white," said Director Hu, "It would be a problem if you did."

Gold Tiger smirked secretly, fully aware that the remark was directed at him because Miao Kui did not hunt at all. *Do you think your innuendo is funny?* He remained reticent. But Director Hu could no longer retain his composure. He stared into Gold Tiger's eyes, "Do you still have an itch to hunt after handing in your rifle?"

"Why do I feel itchy since I'm not infected with lice?"

"But lice can live in mind," responded the quick-thinking director.

Gold Tiger retorted, "So, the police station is also policing lice?" His snappy answer was intentionally provocative. But he didn't care. *I'm not doing anything illegal. You may be powerful, but I'll see what you can do about me!*

Director Hu smirked, "I didn't expect Gold Tiger to be so humorous." Then, his tone turned stern, "Nothing in No. 3 Forest Farm and escape my attention. We may be short of hands in the police station, but our management for a matrix of communities is pretty effective."

Miao Kui kept nodding, "Yes, yes! I haven't heard any public security violations in our No. 3 Forest Farm."

Director Hu said, "We don't have a problem with our public security in No. 3 Forest Farm. The problem is how we can uproot the trend of poaching." He told them that some people were still trading pheasants and partridges in secret. You can order game dishes in almost all the eco restaurants. The police station is determined to solve the problem from its source. I would quit my job if we couldn't stop the unhealthy trend of poaching.

Gold Tiger didn't respond. He thought that Director Hu was doing the right thing. *No trading, no killing. If we can control what we eat, we can end poaching.*

"You've collected all the guns, but why are there people still poaching?"

"So long as we find game dishes in the restaurants, we believe there's still poaching out there, and my mission as a hunter terminator will not be accomplished." Then Director Hu changed the subject abruptly, "Gold Tiger, that Red Mastiff of your is a great hunter."

Gold Tiger quipped, "It's okay to keep a mastiff, isn't it?"

"Of course, it is," said Director Hu, "but you've got to have a permit."

"Everyone keeps dogs in No. 3 Forest Farm. Do they all have permits?" asked Gold Tiger.

"Field dogs are okay without permits. Mastiffs are different cases because they're hunting dogs." Director Hu rose from his feet and added, "Getting a permit doesn't cost you much."

After searching around with his eyes, Director Hu rested them on Gold Tiger. Having been a leader of a reconnaissance company, he was confident of what he could do best. He even proclaimed that he had another pair of eyes behind his head in public.

"I'll go and get it. Red Mastiff is our company's shepherd dog," said Miao Kui.

Director Hu said goodbye and stepped to the door. Then, he turned his head and said to Gold Tiger, "Hey, the Public Security Bureau has destroyed your Red Arrow. They must destroy all the confiscated weapons under regulations."

Gold Tiger shuddered as tears swelled in his eyes, but he pretended nothing had happened. He said, "Red Arrow no longer belongs to me."

"In fact, I think it's a shame, too. Guns aren't law breakers, but men can be."

Gold Tiger opened his mouth but swallowed what he was about to say, knowing whom he meant by stressing the word "men."

After Director Hu's departure, Gold Tiger recalled the past like watching a movie, flashing before his mind's eye frame by frame. Over the past thirty years, he had been in the habit of cleaning his Red Arrow before going to bed. It was a procedure he had followed under any circumstances, even on the Eve of the Chinese New Year. After delivering up Red Arrow, he had no gun to rub so that he would caress Red Mastiff awhile by its doghouse set in the sheep pen. He never denied that he had Red Arrow in his mind when he ran his hands over Red Mastiff.

Miao Kui said, frowning, "What shall we do? What about the lynx-hunting plan?" He had imagined a plan since his return from Lao Mo. And he mentioned it to Gold Tiger from time to time.

Gold Tiger said, "A good hunter always gets excited when hearing tigers or leopards roar. I would have 'washed my hands in a gold basin' if he hadn't come to visit us. By threatening me like that, he did what equals the delivery of a challenge letter."

Miao Kui asked, "So, you've changed your mind?"

"I'll lose face if I didn't have the guts to take his challenge."

"Let me tell you the truth: I've got another shotgun at home," whispered Miao Kui.

"I don't need one," declared Gold Tiger, "Guns aren't the only weapons a hunter can use."

Miao Kui said, "All the hunters in No. 3 Forest Farm know you're a trap expert."

"I may not be an expert," said Gold Tiger, "but descendants of the posthouse ancestors were born with the technique."

"Director Hu doesn't trust you," said Miao Kui, who knew the director's possession of unusual powers as nothing could escape his keen perception. One day, a sheep had been missing, of which the shepherd and he hadn't been aware. Then, Director Hu brought the skinned sheep carcass and the young thief. Only then did he rush to the pen and count the sheep. Sure enough, there was one too few. Miao Kui asked, "How did you know the sheep belonged to our chopsticks company?" Director Hu responded, "You're the only breeder of the Small-tail Han in the four forest farms in the area. Whom else would it belong to?" This case turned Miao Kui into an awe-struck admirer for Director Hu's detective skills.

"If he trusts me, I'll behave by his rules. It's an insult to me for him to suspect me like that," smirked Gold Tiger. "He always says 'Wait and see.' Okay, let's wait and see how powerful he will be."

"We'd better be cautious," said Miao Kui, knowing Director Hu's prowess.

Gold Tiger said, "If used properly, a soft rope is as good as a steel gun."

"Teach me how to set traps, and I'll carry out the lynx-hunting plan."

Gold Tiger broke into a smile. *You can't dare to go to the mountains. How can you carry out the lynx-hunting plan?* But he said, "Okay, I'll teach you. Then, you can catch some rabbits to satisfy your foodie's appetite in the future." Gold Tiger believed that Miao Kui couldn't have caught any lynx even if he learned the trick. A lynx wouldn't be called a lynx if it was easy to fall into a trap.

For days, Gold Tiger taught Miao Kui how to make hunting traps. He imparted everything to him, such as the device to catch an animal by the neck, the foothold trap, strategic locations to set traps, and how to tell various animals from their footprints. After he got the basics, Miao Kui realized that hunting was a profession that took more than marksmanship. The reason was that animals were in hiding while hunters were exposed most of the time. If game animals could use guns, each hunter would have died many times.

Gold Tiger reminded him emphatically, "If we go to the mountains, we should never trap the Class I and II state-protected species. If we did, we would be in big trouble. Gold Tiger knew that Director Hu might give them a way out if they caught animals like wolves, roe deer, wild boars. "He would never let go of us if we should hurt endangered animal species. "I just want to hunt lynxes. I'm not interested in anything else." Gold Tiger responded, "Of course, I know.

If a blind lynx bumped into a trap, that would be its fate, and you aren't to be blamed. Just don't let Director Hu catch us. He's always wanted to play a cat-and-mouse game with us." Gold Tiger made trap loops with steel wire hardly detectable by animals. He experimented with a lamb, and the result was excellent. Animals have a keen sense of smell. Once they detect a peculiar scent, they will balk. Steel wire doesn't give off any odor and can be easily imperceptible.

Miao Kui took a security guard with him when he entered the mountain to test the traps. Gold Tiger stayed put, or he would catch Director Hu's attention because the latter's light brown eyes never rested.

Though he caught nothing in the mountains, Miao Kui ventured farther and farther. To Gold Tiger's alarm, he even reached Sifangtai, a place without signs of human presence.

Sifangtai was an alpine platform with precipices on three sides. The south side was gentle and overgrown with oaks, poplars, and birches. Many legends about Sifangtai circulated in No. 3 Forest Farm because the place was ominous and most likely to cause accidents. A young man named Reckless the Second from the forest farm went hunting one autumn. According to hearsay, he chased a *milu*, a native Chinese deer with features resembling four different animals, and followed it to Sifangtai. The autumn in the Hinggan Range is already chilly. Reckless the Second wore a rabbit-skin hat and an inside-out rabbit fur vest and carried an old-fashioned blunderbuss. As he ran, he sweated profusely. When they got to Sifangtai, the *milu* disappeared. The type of deer is large. Reckless the Second saw it appearing and disappearing in the forests, but it abruptly vanished under his nose. He was milling around close to a precipice, wondering where the *milu* could be, when suddenly, a golden eagle swooped down from the air, reached its sharp claws, and snatched his rabbit-skin hat. At the same time, it tore a palm-size piece of scalp off the top of his head. The gold eagle's sudden attack was nearly fatal. Only by using gunpower did Reckless the Second stop the bleeding. Then, he stumbled all the way home. Anyway, after the incident, few people went to Sifangtai again. There was a stream beneath the cliff on the east side of Sifangtai. Many tall Amur cork trees flanked the stream. Hence, it got its name, Cork Tree Gully. Things in the mountains are always strange: places with treasures are often dangerous. For example, where wild ginseng grows, thee will be guarding pit vipers, and where fine trees grow, there will be nests of protective wasps. The Cork Tree Gully was infested with ticks. They were much more difficult to void than pit vipers. Those bed-bug-sized pests can bore into people's skin stealthily because they cause neither pain nor itching. But they could take away people's lives in their skin. Miao Kui's venture to Sifangtai showed that desire could embolden people.

Returning from Sifangtai, Miao Kui went directly to Gold Tiger's home. He took out a tuft of animal hair and asked if it was from a lynx.

Holding it between his thumb and forefinger, Gold Tiger scrutinized it. He affirmed that it was the hair of a carnivore but was uncertain whether it was lynx hair or not. He said that the color told him it resembled cat hair. He asked Miao Kui where he had found it. "Sifangtai," Miao Kui told him. "It was providence that helped me locate it." He had set a trap on Sifangtai a day before and dreamed of trapping a lynx as big as a leopard. He fired three shots and killed the animal. Waking up, he thought he would have his luck if he went into the mountain that day. So, he inspected the traps he had laid up on Sifangtai. Though he didn't catch any lynx, he spotted this tuft of hair on a Ziziphus jujuba bush.

"It's the signal the Mountain God has given me," said Miao Kui.

Sniffing at the tuft of hair pinched in his hand, again and again, Gold Tiger said, "I'll go to the mountain and take a look."

4

Usually, Gold Tiger wouldn't go to the mountains without his Red Mastiff, which became his indispensable partner after Red Arrow was gone. Director Hu also used Red Mastiff's presence to monitor Gold Tiger as they would appear together all the time. If he couldn't see Red Mastiff, Gold Tiger must have gone to the mountains. From the window on the north side of the second floor of the police station, Director Hu only had to take a look through his binoculars and find Red Mastiff lying there, and he would feel relieved.

Gold Tiger didn't bring Red Mastiff with him so that he could circumvent Director Hu's surveillance when he sneaked into the mountains with Miao Kui at dawn. Miao Kui carried a backpack filled with food and beverage and two raincoats. Gold Tiger liked the bag, saying they could take some mountain produce back in it.

The path leading to Sifangtai was rugged. Gold Tiger fixed his eyes on the dead trees in the forest flanking the trail. Miao Kui was curious. *If you look at the dead trees instead of the path under your feet, what would you find in the dead trees?* Suddenly, Gold Tiger went up to a dead oak tree, stood on tiptoes, and picked a lion's mane mushroom. Then, he found another on a living oak tree seven or eight steps away. Lion's manes are delicacies, best for chicken soup. Miao Kui was envious, but he couldn't find one no matter how wide he opened his eyes. Before long, Gold Tiger collected a few more and said, "Put the mushrooms in the backpack so that we can use them as a present when we go down the mountains." Miao Kui asked, "A present to whom?" Gold Tiger smiled, "You'll know when we get down."

"We're only scouting on this trip to find traces of lynxes," said Gold Tiger.

"I get excited whenever I think of the lynx-hunting plan. It seems we're doing something earthshaking," said Miao Kui. "I feel at ease with you helping me."

"As I said, we're only scouting, not necessarily doing the hunt. I just want to find it and learn about its sphere of activity."

The forest was permeated with moisture and mists. Whiffs of rosin and blueberry smell drifted over from time to time. Gold Tiger enjoyed such air in the woods as if it could filter his lungs and make breathing more pleasant. The grass under the trees was fluffy. Amur grape vines were covered with leaves and pine needles fallen years before. They felt spongy when stepped on. Each step on them would get sprung up. Gold Tiger hadn't been to the depth of the forests since he surrendered his Red Arrow, not to mention Sifangtai. The domains divided up by the hunters were dangerous and laden with many taboos. With a river separating it from the natural reserve on the other side, whoever came here to hunt would be like picking up an ignited firecracker at the gate of a state coffer and bound to get himself into big trouble.

Gold Tiger never considered Director Hu to be a bad guy. He just didn't like him to be so arbitrary and suspicious of him. Director Hu publicly declared that his top mission as the Director of the Police Station of No. 3 Forest Farm was to be a hunter terminator. But he exaggerated his task and didn't take the hunters on the forest farm seriously. *Human civilization has come from hunting. Who can be a hunter terminator? You can only change the way people hunt in your capacity of heading a police station. Do you think we can't hunt without guns? Firearms are only a little over a hundred years old, but humanity's hunting history is over 5,000 years.*

There was no wind in the forest. Only the rustling footfalls were audible. Miao Kui was striding in the front when Gold Tiger behind him blurted out, "Mind you!" Miao Kui halted and turned around to gaze at Gold Tiger, puzzled. Gold Tiger walked up and pointed at the Amur grape vines under his feet. Miao Kui saw a thin wire extended there. Gold Tiger walked closer and examined it, only to find a trap set by some hunter. Gold Tiger pulled out his knife and cut the wire off from below. Then, they resumed their journey. After they walked a hundred steps, Gold Tiger stopped Miao Kui again. This time, it was not a hunting trap but a small camera tied to the branch of a birch tree, with its lens facing an open field in the front. It was a thermal imaging monitor. Gold Tiger said, "It records animals or people passing by day and night."

"Who installed it?" Miao Kui panicked. It meant that he must have been photographed on his multiple trips into the mountains.

"Who else do you think?" Gold Tiger also figured out that it was Director Hu's gadget. He didn't think it was the only monitor Director Hu had installed here. It was so convenient that it could promptly transmit images to a mobile phone. It could monitor wild animals and poachers. "As expected of a reconnaissance company commander, he's resourceful indeed."

Miao Kui looked melancholy, worried that there could also be surveillance monitors on Sifangtai. If so, his lynx-hunting plan would fall flat, even though Gold Tiger had never devised any such plan.

Gold Tiger came to Sifangtai not to hunt lynxes. His move was more of a posture to take a challenge. He would be satisfied with only finding a lynx, not expecting to catch one. It was like a soldier operating a fire-controlled radar to lock on a target. If he could lock on it, he would be able to shoot it down. But it didn't necessarily want to push the firing button. Miao Kui, however, had a different agenda. He dreamed of succeeding in hunting a fox and turning its fur into a hat to stop his baby son from crying at night.

When they arrived at the south slope of Sifangtai, it was about noon. Miao Kui located the Ziziphus jujuba bush where he had found the tuft of animal hair. Gold Tiger examined the location for a moment and called Miao Kui's claim into doubt. Looking around at the terrain and plants, he found only a few young birches, and the grass on the ground was thin while Ziziphus jujuba bushes were flourishing. A place with such an environment wasn't ideal for animals of the Felidae family to frequent. *What would a lynx get into the thorny bush for?* He pulled apart the Ziziphus jujuba bushes with a branch and found a passage under it. It connected to a shallow ditch that led to a cliff several hundred feet high. Inching to the edge of the cliff, he looked down, only to find the grotesque precipitous crags submerged in the tree canopies in a picturesque disorder. To climb down, one had to resort to a rope.

"Lynxes won't build its den in such a place, where their litter would fall from the platform," Gold Tiger asserted. "There must be eagle nests around here. Eagles can catch lynx kittens." He remembered Reckless the Second, whom a golden eagle had injured with its claws.

"Where did the hair come from?"

"Hard to say," Gold Tiger said to himself. *A cunning lynx won't settle where there is no way out.*

Miao Kui suggested setting up a hunting trap here to try their luck. Gold Tiger consented to Miao Kui's proposal. He also wanted to find out what kind of a beast left the tuft of hair, so he placed a wired head-gripping trap in the Ziziphus jujuba bush. He said to himself, "It'll be a record in my hunting career if I can trap a lynx."

After setting the trap, Gold Tiger urged Miao Kui to go back as soon as possible because they would arouse suspicion if they lingered in the mountains for too long.

They walked around on the Sifangtai platform and found a roe deer carcass with a good part of it already eaten by some predators. This discovery proved that there might be large carnivores in the area. Gold Tiger and Miao Kui arrived at the Cork Tree Gulley from the south slope. The gulley was enshrouded with a mist even during the day. The descendants of the ancient posthouses thought that the trees would spew forth smoke and clouds as they grew older. The gully was covered with tall Amur cork trees. There were no trodden paths in the forest, and each step would be hindered by entangling thistles and thorns. At the gully's bottom, both sides of the stream were overgrown with a kind of reed grass known as Deyeuxia purpurea. The source of the Keluo River, this brook with giggling clear water, was teemed with small fish. Gold Tiger spotted wild boar and roe deer poops on the stream's edge. He was confident that there must be predators here because it was common sense that large carnivores follow preys like boars and roe deer wherever they go. Unlike them, the omnivorous black bears are satisfied with acorns, wild berries, and cereal crops. Large and medium-sized carnivores at the top of the food chain may consciously avoid places of human activity and claim the most hidden places as their activity ranges. They may know that humans are their genuine natural enemies.

Opposite the stream in the Cork Tree Gully was a national reserve. Trapping animals there was taboo, of which Gold Tiger was fully aware. Gold Tiger had told Miao Kui the critical points of setting traps: the opening of a den, the path traversed by the game animals, their water source, and where they passed their feces. Generally speaking, laying traps at the opening of an animal den has the most significant success rate. Placing them on the path traversed by the animals comes next. Animals like to take the familiar route. As time goes by, the route eventually becomes an animal path. Setting traps where it narrows is a practical way to catch roe deer and wild boars. Animals need to water, and when they do, they prefer places they consider the safest. Therefore, it'll be easy to get them by laying traps where they drink. Carnivores have strong territorial awareness. They tend to leave traces on the boundaries of their jurisdictions, just like some leaders inspecting the rural areas. Animals use the smell of their feces to warn off intruders. Most animals choose the spots under trees to pass their feces. Therefore, the sites become ideal locations for trapping them. Having learned the tricks, Miao Kui had the urge to try them out. So, he suggested that Gold Tiger lay some traps by the stream. Pointing at the woods on the opposite side, Gold Tiger told Miao Kui, "Trapping animals here won't catch them, but it would certainly plunge us into a prison cell."

Gold Tiger planned to enter the village around five o'clock because Director Hu would not be prowling on the street during mealtime.

Two tall poplar trees stood at the village's entrance in No. 3 Forest Farm, and people customarily called it the "Poplar Gate." Stepping through the "gate," one could see courtyards flanking the main street, separated by wood-plank fences. The houses were of red bricks, roofed with tin tiles. They appeared as orderly as barracks. The village was tranquil at dusk. The setting sun slowly spread like a gigantic yoke on the hillside in the west, blurring the shadows of trees and houses. Gold Tiger and Miao Kui approached the tall poplars when they ran into

Director Hu. The director came out from behind one of the poplars, his left hand holding a walkie-talkie and his right in his pants pocket. His light brown eyes fell upon Miao Kui's backpack. Miao Kui was stunned and stopped walking. "Is Director Hu waiting for someone here?" he asked.

"You've been to the mountains, have you?" Director Hu asked back without responding to his question.

Miao Kui replied, "Since we've got nothing to do, we went to the mountains for a walk."

Director Hu then turned to Gold Tiger, "Nothing to do?"

The expressionless Gold Tiger responded, "We butchered a rooster and meant to stew it into a dish to go with our baijiu. Then, we found that we didn't have any lion's mane left."

"Collecting lion's mane in the mountains?" Director Hu asked, "Would you want to risk mosquito and gadfly bites to collect a few mushrooms?"

Gold Tiger had to show respect for Director Hu, thinking that his light brown eyes could see through people. *Luckily, we didn't catch any lynx. Otherwise, we would've been caught red-handed.* Director Hu walked around the two and found nothing in Gold Tiger's hands before fixing his eyes on the pack on Miao Kui's back. He asked, "You haven't picked a single lion's mane, have you?"

Opening the backpack, Miao Kui took out a few fresh lion's manes and smiled, "Here're a couple for you to fix a soup with. The lion's mane is pretty nourishing."

Director Hu waved "No" with his hand while his eyes still searched the backpack, in which he found nothing else. "It's rare for Sharpshooter to have this leisure to collect lion's manes. The musk deer, roe deer, and other deer in our No. 3 Forest Farm seem to be blessed."

Gold Tiger sensed the innuendo of Director Hu's remark, which he thought to be absent of ill intent. So, he responded in a flat tone, "These deer are indebted to Director Hu. It's Director Hu that has terminated the hunters in No. 3 Forest Farm."

"They should thank the government. The government's good policy has become their protective talisman." Director Hu spoke from the point of view of a public servant.

Gold Tiger said, "If you've got nothing for us, we'll go back to fix our chicken soup."

Director Hu responded, "I haven't anymore. You'd better not have any, either. Or, we'll wait and see."

Miao Kui and Gold Tiger didn't respond. "Wait and see" is Director Hu's pet phrase. With that, he seemed to be ready to let things go.

Director Hu sauntered away. He had appeared from one of the poplars. Gold Tiger turned to look when passing by the tree. He noticed a stump overwhelmed with black nightshade, many of whose berries had blackened, signaling they were ripe. Director Hu had been waiting for their arrival while enjoying the berries. "He knows how to stake out in a comfortable place," Gold Tiger cursed in silence.

Gold Tiger went to see Red Mastiff first and played with it for a while. Miao Kui went to his office, where he asked the chefs in the canteen to fix a few dishes. He also had some beer ready and said, "Alcohol is refreshing." Gold Tiger could perceive something weighing heavily on Miao Kui's mind: he was terrified by Director Hu. *He's faint-hearted, and Direct Hu's innuendos became a load on his mind.*

Gold Tiger sat down and drank beer with Miao Kui. The latter said, "What did Director Hu mean by 'Wait and see'?"

Grabbing a drumstick and munched on it, Gold Tiger responded, "Poaching."

"But you've handed in your rifle."

Gold Tiger gave himself up to gnawing a chicken foot. He relished it because he could savor the aroma of spring onion and Chinese pepper. "I don't know why he doesn't trust us. Perhaps, I'm the Sharp-shooter."

"Director Hu is too ready to suspect. He makes us look like poachers after going to the mountains."

Gold Tiger said, "He's on the right track, isn't he? We did set traps in the mountains. This encounter alone makes me admire him."

Miao Kui said, "Since Direct Hu is keeping an eye on you, we'd better not look for trouble anymore. Let's give up that lynx-hunting plan, shall we?"

Gold Tiger drained a bottle of beer, pounded the empty bottle on the coffee table with a thump, and said with a booming voice, "Was I fed on intimidation to grow up?"

"You want to act in opposition to him?"

"I meant to stop hunting, but he's always suspecting me. If I've stopped, I would be a coward. It's like he's always tantalizing me with meat when I've decided to be on a vegetarian diet. If I don't take it, it would mean I've got bad teeth."

Miao Kui nodded, "I know you're deliberately annoying him."

"I can annoy him, but I don't want to be involved in lynx hunting," said Gold Tiger. "Lynxes have long been listed as endangered animals under state protection. I wouldn't hunt them even if I had my Red Arrow."

Tears swelled in Miao Kui's eyes. "I don't want to make it hard on you, Bro."

"But there are lynxes on Sifangtai indeed. I trust my intuition," declared Gold Tiger.

5

Miao Kui believed in what Gold Tiger had said. As always, his information was accurate: There were lynxes on Sifangtai.

Miao Kui found a hunter named Big Brother Gao in No. 4 Forest Farm, promising him a fabulous sum of money if he could catch a lynx for him. Big Brother Gao said it was too tricky to hunt a lynx. Besides, he had no gun. Miao Kui promised that he would manage to find him one and asked him to stay at home, and he would tell him what to do. They agreed to keep the deal to themselves. Big Brother Gao knows Gold Tiger, so he asked, "There's a Sharpshooter in your No. 3 Forest Farm. Why don't you ask him for help?" Miao Kui said, "He's so famous that he would catch the police's attention."

Miao Kui went to Sifangtai to inspect his traps almost every day. He found it empty each time, not even a rabbit in them. The security guard accompanying him reminded him that he had heard that one couldn't inspect the traps one had laid every day. A round of inspection every three or five days would do. But Miao Kui was anxious. He wished that he could catch a lynx one day. Ji'ao's infantile anorexia was worsening, vomiting whatever he ate. Miao Kui called Lao Mo, telling him that lynxes were challenging to hunt, and asked if alternatives like hats of rabbit or raccoon fur would be as effective. Lao Mo responded bluntly, "Monsters and ghosts are smarter than humans. You'll court death if you're making fools of them!" Lao Mo's words dispelled Miao Kui's eagerness to find an alternative. He set his mind on carrying out the plan to hunt lynxes.

Gold Tiger knew What was on Miao Kui's mind, saying, "You can't trap a lynx even if you found its whereabouts. To a hunter, capturing a lynx is like winning the Olympic event of the modern pentathlon. A hunter who has caught a lynx can swagger proudly in the whole forest farm.

One day, Miao Kui came down from Sifangtai fatigued. So many futile attempts sapped his confidence, doubting if trapping was an effective way of getting a lynx. The accompanying security guard was also disappointed: *Hunting should have been exciting, but what's the fun of going to the mountains every day if we can't catch a sparrow?* Miao Kui took a water bottle out of his backpack and sat down under an old oak tree to rest. Some black honey bees were buzzing around the oak tree. One of them landed on his head. He raised his hand and shooed the insect away. Suddenly, he spotted a young tabby lying on a branch above him. The security guard sitting on the meadow also caught sight of it. Pointing at it, he shouted, "Boss, there's a kitten above your head!"

Miao Kui stared at the kitten closely as the latter gazed back with widened eyes, terribly alarmed. Its eyes looked adorable with large and round eyes. Miao Kui said, "Its owner may have abandoned it. A poor thing! Let's take it back and keep it."

The security guard climbed up the tree as the kitten pawed at him in resistance. Since it was too small and probably unweaned, the guard quickly captured it. Miao Kui unfastened the backpack and placed the kitten in it. The young animal was so docile that it neither struggled nor cried. The two men went down the mountain and returned to the village.

When Miao Kui came back, Gold Tiger watched people play chess on the small plaza in front of the police station. Miao Kui called him, asking him to go to his office. After rushing back, Gold Tiger looked at the kitten in a carton and was stunned, "Where did you catch it?"

"We got it from a tree. I think an adult cat must have abandoned it," said Miao Kui.

"What do you mean by an adult cat and a kitten? It's a lynx kitten! Where's the adult one?"

Miao Kui was pleasantly surprised. He had never seen a lynx kitten and thought it was an abandoned feral cat. After Gold Tiger identified it, he held the lynx kitten up and scrutinized it. He asked with bewilderment, "Why do you think it's a young lynx?"

Gold Tiger told him that lynx and feral cat kittens were different in two ways. One is their tails, and the other is their ears. A lynx kitten's tail is thick and short, whereas a feral cat's is thin and long. A lynx kitten has tufted outlines on the tips of its ears, while the hair on the feral cat kitten's ears is evenly distributed. A lynx's litter consists of only two kittens, and their mother takes excellent care of them. Usually, a hunter can only catch an adult lynx if he is lucky enough. But he'll find it exceptionally challenging to get a young one. That's because a mother lynx always hide its litter in a highly safe place.

Miao Kui related how he found this lynx kitten. Gold Tiger concluded that it must have been separated from its mother. The female lynx most likely had two babies and took one away first before returning to retrieve the other in a moment. But just at that juncture, Miao Kui took away the other one. The mother lynx must be mad with anxiety. Gold Tiger believed that the discovery of the kitten was a bad sign: the lynxes on Sifangtai might be migrating. Miao Kui's frequent visits must have disturbed them.

"With the kitten in our hands, we'll eventually catch the female lynx," said Miao Kui, "Where shall we keep this little thing? We can't afford to let Director Hu find it."

"If he found it, we'll be in deep trouble," said Gold Tiger.

How to deal with the lynx kitten became a thorny problem. After discussion, they decided to hide it.

"Where to?" Miao Kui was at a loss. "Besides, it grows bigger with each passing day. Fire will eventually burn through a paper wrap."

"Put it in the sheep pen, and we'll decide what to do next." After saying so, Gold Tiger realized that he had become Miao Kui's accomplice and gave Director Hu a handle. Only Heavens knows whether he would be in trouble or not. He seemed to have seen Director Hu's light brown eyes with their spine-chilling look.

"Okay, let's hide it in the sheep pen." Miao Kui also considered it the only resort they had.

While Gold Tiger was worried, Miao Kui looked extraordinarily excited. After all, he found the whereabouts of lynxes, which had opened the door to the lynx-hunting plan. Gold Tiger carried the lynx kitten to the sheep pen. Miao Kui called Big Brother Gao and told him that he had the gun ready. He asked Gao to remain prepared, and he would let him know when they went to the mountains to hunt lynxes.

When he got to the pen, Gold Tiger settled the kitten in the innermost section of the enclosure. The kitten kept mewing and didn't quiet down until he found a milk bottle and fed it a small bag of sheep milk.

Director Hu came the following day as was expected. Red Mastiff always barked at him but not furiously. It sounded like a warning or tip-off. Hearing Red Mastiff barking, Gold Tiger came out of the sheep pen and gave the director a lukewarm greeting, "Morning!"

"Morning," Director Hu returned the greeting and looked into the sheep pen outside the fence. There were over a hundred Small-tail Han sheep in the sheep pen, some standing and others lying, but all were calm and unruffled. Director Hu mocked, "You've been working pretty hard to raise your sheep these days."

"We've got nothing to do anyway. So, we're here to clean the pen." Gold Tiger guessed right: Director Hu had been keeping an eye on him. The director came so early because he had found something usual.

"It's great you're cleaning the pen. Cleaning it won't get you in trouble," said Director Hu as he lit a cigarette and sat down against the enclosing wall.

"We'll be in trouble even if we don't clean it," said Gold Tiger in a matter-of-fact manner.

"It's great you're not in trouble," said Director Hu as he drew a circle in the air with his fingers holding the cigarette. "To be frank, I'm worried about you the most because you're Sharpshooter after all."

Gold Tiger burst into laughter, "You may rest assured. Without a gun, 'Sharpshooter' is nothing but a name."

Director Hu pinched the cigarette off, turned around, and looked at the sheep pen. He then walked to Red Mastiff's doghouse and inspected it for a while. "Tether it securely so it won't hurt anyone," he said.

"Red Mastiff is well trained. It bites bad guys only."

"But bad guys won't have a sign to identify themselves in public," said Director Hu. "Well, come to the police station and get a permit as soon as possible. You must keep your dog legally."

Gold Tiger nodded. Brother the Sixth had called him and urged him to get the permit for Red Mastiff. He questioned Brother the Sixth, "Every household has a dog in our forest farm, but who has gotten a permit?" Brother the Sixth responded, "Director Hu says you're different from others. You're on top of the list of people who need monitoring." Knowing that Brother the Sixth was carrying out the director's orders, he didn't want to be hard on him. So, he promised him that he would find time to get the permit. He said, "To get a permit is like getting a marriage license, and to do so, I must choose an auspicious day."

Before he left, Director Hu said, "Misfortune comes out and also goes into the mouth. It doesn't pay to eat game and get locked up in jail." Gold Tiger retorted, "I'm a hunter alright, but I don't have a penchant for hunted meat. I hunted only for excitement."

"Good," nodded Director Hu. "You won't suffer from retribution if you aren't greedy." With that, he expanded his chest and walked out.

Gold Tiger could tell that Director Hu must have sensed something. Otherwise, he wouldn't have come to the sheep pen early in the morning with his searching eyes. Miao Kui asked, "Did he find out the lynx kitten?" Gold Tiger responded, "Not necessarily. If he found the kitten in the sheep pen, he wouldn't have left like that." That night, Gold Tiger was sleepless, somewhat feeling uneasy. He fell asleep only after he got up at midnight and drank some baijiu.

Going to bed with the help of alcohol, one sleeps early and gets up early. The first crow of a rooster woke Gold Tiger up. The July morning air in the forest farm usually was sweet and pleasant. But Gold Tiger smelled blood, and the odor was so strong that he could sense a thick salty stench. A hunter's senses are incredibly keen. The scent gave him a feeling of an ill omen. Throwing his coat over his back, he strode to the sheep pen, thinking it should be safe with Red Mastiff on guard. Its barking was loud enough to wake up the whole forest farm so that no one would dare steal the sheep, not to mention the good public order. The descendants of the ancient posthouses had still adhered to the tradition of not bolting their doors when they were asleep at night.

As he approached the pen, he found something wrong. Red Mastiff was lying still 20 feet away from the doghouse, with the iron chain pulled tight. Typically, it would come up to greet him joyfully when hearing his footsteps. *What happened today?* He called it, but there was no response. He called again, but Red Mastiff still didn't budge. He dashed over and crouched down, only to find it dead.

"Who did it?" Director Hu was the first to come into his mind. *Did he kill Red Mastiff only because I don't have a permit?* But he quickly reversed the judgment. *Director Hu won't do things like this. He could play fair and square and confiscate it instead of destroying it. But who else? Since Red Mastiff neither fought back nor barked and died without a whimper, the only cause of death must be poison.*

After careful examination, he found that Red Mastiff's neck was bitten off. Judging from the deep wound, he concluded that a single strike had killed it. He suddenly thought of something. He leaped into the pen's enclosure, rushed to the last section of the sheep pen, and looked for the lynx kitten. Alas, it was gone! Although the sheep pen's door was latched, the vent window had always been open. The kitten must have been taken out of it. He realized that the mother lynx had come to its baby's rescue and attacked Red Mastiff. It was the iron chain tying Red Mastiff that made its assault successful. Otherwise, the lynx couldn't have been so lucky. The traces on site showed that the female lynx must have pounced on Red Mastiff from behind and bit its neck. Tears streamed down and fell on the hand caressing Red

Mastiff's body. The lynx couldn't have gotten to Red Mastiff's neck if he had put the stainless steel collar on it. He felt he had been unfair to Red Mastiff. *It's only one year old, but it's dead before it gets a chance to give a full play to its ability and talent.*

"The damn lynx!" He cursed with anger. "If you tried to save your baby, why could you go to the pen directly? Why did you attack and kill Red Mastiff? It was chained so that it couldn't block or chase you. You may just have taken your baby with you."

Miao Kui hurried over and couldn't resign to the tragic reality that Red Mastiff was killed and the lynx kitten was missing. "How could this be? How could this be? The lynx was quicker in action than the CIA. Its opponent was none other than a mastiff!"

"It's entirely my fault. I should've unleashed Red Mastiff," said Gold Tiger with terrible guilt.

"The lynx was pretty fierce!" Miao Kui looked at Red Mastiff's wound.

Now, don't blame me for retaliation!" Gold Tiger rose to his feet, looked at the mountain forests in the distance, and said with clenched teeth, "You forced me to take action!" He stooped down, unleased Red Mastiff's chain, took off his jacket and covered its head with it.

"Get me a spade. I'll bury it in the forest," said Gold Tiger. "Without the permit, Red Mastiff isn't registered with the police station."

Miao Kui handed him a spade, along with a blanket. They wrapped Red Mastiff in it and carried it into the mountains, where they buried it under a catalpa bungei tree. Gold Tiger heaped a grave mound and placed a stone slab of the size of a large brick horizontally in front of it as a unique symbol of his commemoration. He then asked Miao Kui not to tell anyone about Red Mastiff's death. "If someone asks about it, tell him that we have got it adopted," he added.

6

Gold Tiger would hunt the lynx on Sifangtai. "I've made up my mind," he said.

Gold Tiger was meticulous when he set his traps, disguised and measured to the millimeters. Miao Kui now realized why his traps performed practically no function: Only fools could have fallen victim to the traps set in a conspicuous place. Setting traps is a process of studying the game: its size, habit, path, and taboos. Only with a deep understanding of the factors can a hunter increase the success rate of his traps. Miao Kui felt that, though Gold Tiger had shared his perceptions with Miao Kui, he had learned only a superficial knowledge of what Gold Tiger knew. *Trap laying is a science!*

After arriving at Sifangtai, Gold Tiger was not ready to set the traps. Instead, he carefully examined the traces of animals everywhere as if he were a mine detection engineer. He didn't destroy the surrounding vegetation, nor did he drive trap-fixing wedges into the ground. He would rather use whatever came handy naturally, such as the trees or crags. Traps set this way were hard to discover. Mai Kui thought of the traps he had laid before. The trampled grass around his devices would naturally alert the animals.

Gold Tiger's initial success was catching a rabbit. It was dark gray, weighing over two kilograms. When he found it, it was still alive, only that it had passed out. He unfastened the rabbit and placed it under the shade of a tree. He didn't want to bring it back because he knew Director Hu was lying in wait at the village entrance. If the director found game animals with him, his plan to catch the lynx would fall flat. The rabbit came to before long. It looked around in panic and limped away.

The presence of the rabbit worried Gold Tiger because it indicated that there wouldn't be its natural enemies here any time soon. Naïve as they were, rabbits had a keen sense of smell, and their noses were constantly wiggling and twitching. The scent of any carnivore would scare them away. *Is my intuition wrong?* His judgment that there were lynxes in the area was based on the lynx poop he had found on Sifangtai during his previous visit with Miao Kui. Lynx feces are similar to wolf's. They are both light-colored, but the wolf poops are obviously broken, whereas the lynx's are olive-shaped, which is characteristic of feline excrement. Gold Tiger had checked many trees in the area, specifically the tall dead ones, hoping to discover the tree holes used by lynxes as their hideouts. But the trees were all healthy without holes large enough for lynxes. It was apparent that the lynx kitten was a stranger to Sifangtai.

"You want to play hide-and-seek with me, eh? Let's wait and see," he murmured to himself.

To avoid Director Hu's attention, he would drive a flock of sheep to the mountains. When they arrived at the meadow, he put the security guard in charge of the sheep. He and Miao Kui would rush to Sifangtai. They brought a home-raised hen of the Plymouth Rock species with them this time.

"Lynxes need baits," he told Miao Kui. "Of course, we won't allow the female lynx to eat the chicken. My wife needs it to lay eggs."

They decided on the best location to hunt the lynx. It was in a grass-covered ravine by one of Sifangtai's precipices. There were traces of wild animals walking at the bottom of the ditch, with lots of the grass trampled down. Gold Tiger set a trap in a depression at one end of the ravine. It was surrounded by waist-deep Ziziphus jujuba bushes. He tied the hen to a branch in the center of the bushes and fastened the trap to the base of a white birch tree with an iron wire. A lynx wasn't powerful enough to break the birch tree. After he finished, Gold Tiger whispered to the cackling Plymouth Rock, "Don't be afraid. I'll take you home with me after this."

Afterward, he laid another trap at the edge of the cliff. "I've sensed your odor, and I'll get you for sure," Gold Tiger raised his muttering voice. "A life for a life. Red Mastiff can't die in vain!"

"Where shall we lie in wait?" asked Miao Kui.

"At home, of course. We'll be back for the inspection." When leaving Sifangtai, Gold Tiger turned around and looked at the Plymouth Rock hen, whispering again, "I know you can't escape the way you're tied, just like Red Mastiff. If I hadn't fastened it, it wouldn't have lost its life. But what else can I do? If I grudge giving you up, I can't capture the lynx." He had told Miao Kui that Red Mastiff's loose skin could have stood a few bites by the lynx if he had not been chained. "Like the Shar-Pei, its skin is bite-proof," he explained.

Driving the flock of sheep to the village entrance, they saw the "Poplar Gate" from a distance. Gold Tiger thought that Director Hu must be sitting there. Passing the "gate," they found no trace of him. They were wondering in surprise while looking back when, suddenly, a motorcycle vroomed over behind them. *Why is Director Hu going to the mountains on a motorcycle? Why didn't we find him where he used to be?* Though extremely suspicious, Gold Tiger turned around and walked into the village as if nothing had happened.

The motorcycle braked to a stop. With his legs on the ground, Director Hu asked, "Hey Gold Tiger, why does the shepherd team suddenly have one member too many?"

"He tagged along so we could have more fun when we played 'Cockfighting,' a card game. Miao Kui lied to find an excuse for the security guard.

"Where's your Red Mastiff, Gold Tiger? Why haven't we seen him for days?" Director Hu didn't know that a lynx had killed it.

"Well, Red Mastiff has gone to where it belongs," responded Gold Tiger.

"Where does it belong?" Director Hu wasn't satisfied with the answer.

"Red Mastiff is a thoroughbred, so someone borrowed it to father his puppies." Gold Tiger came up with a provisional response, which was more acceptable. All mastiff keepers loan their males ones to make some money.

Director Hu stopped asking more questions. But he was still suspicious of their intent to go to the mountains. *Playing the "Cockfighting" card game in the mountain? Are you kidding a child?* Focusing his eyes on the canvas duffle bag carried on the back of the security guard. "Is it bulging with lion's manes again?"

The security guard showed Director Hu the contents of the bag. The latter glanced at it and didn't find any game. There was only a small engineer spade, which didn't count as a weapon. He made a warning remark, "I always feel you're planning something. You mustn't take offense at my frankness, but since we run into each other every day, don't let me catch you red-handed." With that, he gave the motorcycle's accelerator a good push and vroomed away.

Watching the motorcycle speeding away, Gold Tiger knew that Director Hu's suspicion was growing. He must have found out that only the security guard had been herding the sheep, and their trips to Sifangtai had caught his attention. He thought that if they captured a lynx, they must skin and dispose of it in the mountains. Bringing it back would allow the police to catch them with the illegal game.

To avoid catching Director Hu's attention, they went to the mountains without the flock the following day. Gold Tiger and Miao Kui stole out of the village early dawn, hoping to come back early.

A round trip to Sifangtai took about three hours. Thus, they could return to the village before nine in the morning.

They were shocked when they came to the location where they had set the trap: the Plymouth Rock hen was gone. The feathers and bloodstain on the grass indicated that some animal had eaten the chicken. However, the steel-wire trap in the Ziziphus jujuba bushes was intact.

"Great!" muttered Gold Tiger, "What an intelligent and agile animal!"

He twisted his nose and smelled a whiff of urine. He looked around and found something gray flashing a few dozen steps away in the oak tree grove and vanished instantly.

"I saw it," said he, swallowing, "The animal is watching us, too."

Seeing nothing, Miao Kui scanned the surroundings with his wide-opened eyes.

"Don't have to look for it," said Gold Tiger, "Let's go. We'll come back tomorrow."

Miao Kui glanced at the empty depression and sighed, "Poor hen."

The two came back so early that they didn't bump into the mysteriously unpredictable Director Hu. But Gold Tiger could sense a pair of light brown eyes gazing at him. He didn't turn around, saying to himself, "Are you tired of playing this childish cat-and-mouse game with us?"

7

On Sifangtai, an area of less than a hectare, Gold Tiger had lost three chickens. He had bought two red roosters besides the Plymouth Rock hen. With attractive colors and loud crows, roosters were more appealing to the game animals. But all three had succumbed, leaving the depression covered with their feathers. The steel-wire trap was still intact.

"What a difficult lynx to deal with!" Staring at the small depression surrounded by the Ziziphus jujuba bushes, Gold Tiger fumed with anger.

Miao Kui was more anxious, thinking they were feeding the lynxes for nothing. Last night, he called Big Brother Gao, telling him there was hard evidence of lynx activities on Sifangtai, only that it disappeared after it popped its head briefly. Miao Kui wasn't sure about laying traps. The gray animal wouldn't have escaped if Gold Tiger had had a rifle. But Gold Tiger insisted on not using guns, saying that the use of firearms would turn this hunting adventure into a fundamentally different matter. Miao Kui was aware that Gold Tiger might not be afraid of Director Hu, but he tried to avoid confronting him. Gold Tiger had pledged that he had made it a rule that he would never use a firearm after surrendering his Red Arrow. "A rule is made not to be broken," said Gold Tiger, "It's like the rule about not hunting foxes and weasels laid down by the hunters' ancestors. Rules are based on previous lessons. We'll suffer if we don't follow the rules." Miao Kui understood that the trauma of being locked up in a dark cell still lingered with Gold Tiger. He planned to exclude Gold Tiger from the plan as soon as the latter found the trace of the lynx. Then, he would ask Big Brother Gao to hunt it in the mountains.

Gold Tiger's trap on the edge of the cliff caught a wolf by its neck so that it was hanging from the precipice. The wolf was stiff when it was found. Golden Tiger pulled the dead wolf up. It frightened Miao Kui out of his wits and sent him trembling nonstop. The wolf's brown hair was somewhat mottled. Its teeth were bare, eyes wide open, and tongue drooped out on the side of its mouth. Gold Tiger unfastened the wolf's body from the trap, dug a hole in the ground not far away with the engineering spade, and buried it in it. Hunting wolves was also forbidden. They would be in trouble if Director Hu found it out. Gold Tiger asked Miao Kui to get a hunting license, but Director Hu rejected his application, saying that the superior authorities brought hunting under strict control. Application for hunting licenses had been suspended for all the ethnic groups except for a quota of a small number of the Oroqen and Evenki people. No one knew whether it was Director Hu's intent. His purpose was clear anyway: rendering Sharpshooter obsolete once and for all.

"I wanted the wolfskin very much," said Miao Kui, who felt it was a shame to bury the wolf with it. "Everyone says it can exorcize evil spirits when used to cover seats."

People of the forest farms like to use wolfskin as seat pads, like the people in a particular country who make it into collars of down coats. It's nothing but a habit. Saying that it can exorcize evil spirits is a bit far-fetched. Gold Tiger knew that they would never escape Director Hu's light brown eyes if they had brought the wolfskin back. Then, all their efforts in carrying out the lynx-hunting plan would come to nothing. Rather than telling Miao Kui about its effect on the plan, Gold Tiger explained, "Wolfskin sheds hair in summer. If you want it, we can always get it in winter."

Watching Gold Tiger burying the dead wolf reminded Miao Kui of the scene of interring Red Mastiff the other day. They wouldn't have let that gray animal get away if it had been alive. He had heard from a veteran hunter that dogs were indispensable to hunting. When the ancestors created the word hunting with the "dog" radical, it made a lot of sense. [6]

"The moon will be full tomorrow night," said Gold Tiger. "We'll spend the night on Sifangtai."

Miao Kui said, "I'm fine if we stay as many nights as you want. Is it necessary to change the bait?"

"Nope. It has gotten used to it."

---

[6] The Chinese character for "hunting" is 猎, which is a compound composed of the root word 昔 and the radical 犭 deriving from the character 犬, which means "dog."

After returning, Miao Kui went to a chicken peddler and selected a rooster. I was walking back carrying the bird in a PP woven bag when he came across Director Hu. The latter stopped him and asked what he was carrying. Seeing the rooster, the director asked, knitting his brows, "You've bought several chickens in the past few days. What're you up to?" Miao Kui stood in a momentary daze and then explained that he had gotten a folk prescription: stewing a rooster with fresh lion's manes to relieve cold syndrome of the stomach and asthenia of the spleen. So, not only did he buy chickens, but he also went to collect lion's manes in the mountains in the past few days. He said, "It's harder and harder to find lion's manes." Miao Kui told two lies, which anticipated Director Hu's next question that he didn't have to ask.

"I wondered why you and Sharpshooter had been going to the mountain so often. It turned out that you've been collecting lion's mane mushrooms. I'm afraid you've depleted the lion's manes in our No. 3 Forest Farm. But I must warn you against doing anything illegal."

Miao Kui shrugged, "What illegal things can we do?"

Tilting his head sideways, Director Hu said, "Tell Sharpshooter, I've got eyes behind my head. Tell him to forget about hunting."

Miao Kui felt his heart thumping hard. Director Hu's light brown eyes were scary as if his look were a skin-penetrating needle.

Miao Kui told Gold Tiger everything Director Hu had said when he returned. Gold Tiger chuckled, thinking it would be abnormal for Director Hu not to be suspicious.

"Let's put off going to the mountains to the afternoon tomorrow. Gold Tiger said, "I've asked Brother the Sixth. He said Director Hu has a habit of taking a nap after lunch. He usually wakes up at one and a half. So, let's go to the mountains at one o'clock."

The two drank tea calmly in the morning. Gold Tiger knew that Director Hu could see what was going on in the office with his binoculars. Miao Kui pulled the curtain apart and opened the window. After lunch, they went out of the village separately and met after passing the "Poplar Gate."

After arriving at Sifangtai, they tied the rooster in the same depression and set the steel-wire trap. Miao Kui asked why they always set the trap here in the depression and if they could choose another place. Gold Tiger explained setting traps was like angling fish. "You can't change the location. Unlike humans who always look for a change, animals prefer their old routes." This time, after laying the trap, Gold Tiger set a triggerable lasso beside the rooster so that it could catch the animal when it touched off the trigger by trying to grab the chicken. After everything was in order, Gold Tiger patted the rooster gently, saying, "If you succeed in helping us, I'll keep you for the rest of your life."

At dusk, the symphony of chirping insets and birds in harmony with the roaring animals turned Sifangtai into a concert stage. Owls hooted from time to time, giving people the goosebumps as they sometimes sounded like a coughing old man, sometimes like a crying newborn. Heavy fog permeated the forest. It was time for carnivores, which had regained their energy during the day, to stretch themselves and come out foraging. Gold Tiger found an old oak tree, on which they could put up for the night. There are two advantages to staying overnight in a tree: a wide field of vision that makes surveillance easier and a safe place to defend against wolves' sudden attacks. The tall oak tree had multiple crotches. Gold Tiger asked Miao Kui to sleep on a higher crotch while he chose one beneath it. The arrangement made it easy for them to react to any dangerous situation. They couldn't apply insect repellent to their bodies, so they brought a beekeeping veil. Wearing them, they would be free from mosquito stings. However, they interfered with their view so that the area with the depression looked hazy under the moon.

The night was getting deeper. The moonlight cut the foliage of the oak tree into pieces. To keep themselves from falling from the trees, they fasten themselves by the waist to the tree as electricians secure themselves to electric poles with their body belts. Miao Kui brought his super bright flashlight, which Gold Tiger had recommended. *It's more effective to drive away wolves than blunderbusses,* he said.

With a bit of scare, Miao Kui said, "Will there be wolves at night? We caught a wolf last time, didn't we."

"It would be a lone wolf if there will be any because there won't be packs of wolves in the forest," said Gold Tiger. "How can you fear a wolf when you dare to catch a lynx?"

Miao Kui responded, "We don't have guns. You have only a knife, and I have my engineering spade. What hunters are equipped like us?" Miao Kui, holding his arms, was worried about the appearance of beasts of prey. He feared that they two couldn't deal with them.

"Then, you shouldn't have come," chaffed Gold Tiger, "Hunting is gambling."

Miao Kui simpered, "I'm scared of nothing with you here." The oak leaves emitted whiffs of sweety aromas at night, and it got more intense as the night deepened. It was the first time Gold Tiger discovered this phenomenon after decades of hunting. This pleasant scent intoxicated him as he appreciated the beauty of the night. Insects like mosquitoes came to harass them from time to time. But they could only buzz outside their veils. After a while, they flew away as they couldn't get anything. Miao Kui, a bit tired, nodded into a doze and then began to snore. Fortunately, his heavy breathing was gentle enough not to disturb any game animals. So, Gold Tiger didn't bother to shake him awake.

As the chirping of the insects died down, Gold Tiger felt a bit drowsy, and his eyelids weighed heavier and heavier. The past flashed frame by frame in front of his mind's eye. He had trapped a wild boar thirty years before. It was a sow with a farrow. The sow was caught in the waist, unable to move forward or backward. The litter of piglets kept crying around it. He estimated that the sow was more than 150 kilograms. It could trade for a brand-name bicycle, which he had dreamed of having for years. It's the consensus of the hunters in No. 3 Forest Farm to kill a trapped boar. It was because, not long before, a veteran hunter of the farm who went to the mountain encountered a boar in heat. The animal bumped him and broke five of his ribs. The veteran hunter told his visiting fellow hunters that they must kill the boar they trapped because it would hurt them if they didn't. Now that they had captured such a giant sow, Gold Tiger would, put it to death. He raised his rifle and took his aim. The sow saw his move, her eyes filled with hopelessness. After staring into his eyes for a moment, it suddenly fell on all fours. The piglets quickly ran to their mother's front and formed a half-circle to protect it. The curious Gold Tiger wondered why these little pigs would do this and why the sow would drop on its knees. He didn't pull the trigger because he would have hurt the farrow if he had done so. And killing young animals was Hunters' taboo. He put away his gun, pulled out his knife, and cut off the hemp rope that fixed the trap, letting the sow run with its babies. At that time, he had thought that a sow with a farrow didn't count as a lone boar and that his act wouldn't go against the veteran hunter's appeal.

He remembered killing a black bear. It was this feat that made him known as Sharpshooter.

The incident happened in early winter. In the Cork Tree Gully, the stream wasn't frozen yet. The grass was all withered. He met with a hunter from elsewhere. The hunter had a blunderbuss and came to hunt pheasants. A blunderbuss is good for hunting wild birds with a large killing area. They didn't talk and kept a distance. Everyone living in the mountains knows that people are more dangerous than the beasts. Anything could happen between two total strangers with firearms if one harbors an ill intent. Both Gold Tiger and that hunter knew the logic. They spotted simultaneously the black bear that came to water by the stream. The bear was as big as a bull and as black as coal. Usually, experienced hunters would shun it because they could do nothing about such a colossal monster without a proper weapon. Gold Tiger was ready to leave, but he saw that hunter stand where he was in hesitance. He didn't seem to evade the bear. Gold Tiger wondered why he would risk his life by challenging the beast with a blunderbuss. But the hunter appeared possessed. He pulled out the cap that had stopped the muzzle, emptied the small iron pellets, and replaced them with larger ball pellets. He was either crazy or inexperienced. The enraged black bear won't give you a second chance to fill your gun with pellets if you miss the first shot. Gold Tiger wanted to stop him, but he remembered the hunters' convention that he must refrain from saying too much. A hunter concentrated on getting a game animal hates interference the most, especially a stranger. He can turn his gun at an interrupter if a misunderstanding should arise between the two. Gold Tiger couldn't stand seeing something extremely tragic happening before his eyes. He turned and went deep into the thick forest, hiding behind a tall tilia tree. Just then, he heard "bang!" The hunter fired and hit the bear's shoulder. The beast twirled around first and then jumped high. A blunderbuss would emit a cloud of lingering smoke after being fired. It was this smoke cloud that betrayed the hunter's position. The black bear threw itself on the hunter like lightning. With a single swoop of its paw, it sent the hunter rolling to a distance. The blunderbuss was tossed up in the air, drew an arc, and fell on the grass. "Good Heavens," Gold Tiger blurted out. What came next would be the bear crushing and tearing its victim. That is how a bear kills its captive: slapping it with its paw, crushing it with its bottom, and tearing it with its teeth. Just imagine a beast as heavy as a bull weighing down a person. It would undoubtedly smash his bones doom his life. The bear's pawing severely injured the man, who doubled up on the grass, convulsing. The priority now was to save his fellow hunter. He couldn't bear seeing him die in the bear's mouth. Gold Tiger hopped from behind the tilia tree, roaring, and pulled back the bolt of his rifle. His loud outburst attracted the black bear's attention. It was no longer interested in the unconscious man. Turning around, the bear stood up and gave a loud growl of anger. A bear stands on its feet when it's furious beyond description. It's a posture of protest and a precursor of a fierce onslaught. Taking advantage of the bear's standing posture, Gold Tiger aimed at the tuft of white hair on the bear's chest and pulled the trigger. The clump of white hair indicates the location of the beast's heart. No one knows why the Creator marks the most vulnerable part of this animal with the tuft of white hair. Veteran hunters of posthouse descent say that it was the gift of the Heavens to the hunters. In the era of the archers, this white hair was the bull's-eye of the target. Killing a bear with a single small-caliber bullet made Gold Tiger famous, and his nickname "Sharpshooter" became a legend in the forest farms. The hunter, who had suffered a comminuted fracture in his left arm in the paw of the black bear, quit hunting. He was from Huma County,

Heilongjiang Province. Since then, he came to visit him with two bottles of sorghum baijiu every year.

The moon turned to the west of Sifangtai. The Ziziphus jujuba bushes began to look hazy. Gold Tiger fell half asleep. He felt as if he saw Director Hu walking up and kicking away the rooster, giving him a shudder. Then, Director Hu disappeared like a stringed puppet. He opened his eyes and took another look. A grayish thing was approaching the Ziziphus jujuba bushes quietly. He felt greatly bucked, and his heart thumped faster. He took off the veil and rubbed his eyes. "It must be you," he said to himself. "If you can escape this time, I'll take you as my master!"

The grayish thing stayed motionless by the Ziziphus jujuba bushes, seemingly to observe the rooster.

Gold Tiger got down the tree noiselessly and inched forward a few steps, arching his back. He wanted to see more clearly. He approached a white birch and peered carefully at the depression with the help of the moonlight. He could tell that the grayish mass was a dog-like animal, something like a badger, a wolf, or a lynx, too. He already concluded that it was precisely the cunning lynx, whatever it resembled. Suddenly, the grayish mass jumped over the Ziziphus jujuba bushes and pounced on the rooster. He was thrilled, "Got it!"

But something strange happened. The grayish mass jumped out of the Ziziphus jujuba bushes, darted to the precipice along the shallow gully, and vanished there.

"The animal is miraculous!"

The commotion startled Miao Kui awake. He jumped off and asked, "What happened?"

Gold Tiger didn't respond. He went directly to Ziziphus jujuba bushes instead. Shining upon the depression with his super bright flashlight, they found the trap triggered already, and the lasso was around the rooster's neck, which was broken by an animal's teeth. If it had not been fastened securely, it would have been taken away by that animal.

"It was hard to deal with. I've underestimated it." Gold Tiger picked up the dead rooster, whose legs were still twitching constantly.

Since he had been asleep, Miao Kui missed the scene of the game animal trying to catch the rooster. He regretted snoozing too heavily. Gold Tiger's words reminded him, and he said, "It wouldn't have slipped away if we had had our gun."

Gold Tiger put down the rooster, placed his hands over his hips, and growled, "I'll catch it without a firearm."

"Don't you think the animal has sensed the trap we've laid?"

Gold Tiger nodded, "It's ribbing us. I'll play with it to the end."

An owl hooted in the forest. It was funny. The hoot seemed to mock the two for busying themselves overnight for nothing. Gold Tiger muttered, "The owl didn't cry earlier or later. Its timing bodes ill!"

"Does it come again tonight?

Gold Tiger responded, "It has a good memory. We can't use dead chickens anymore."

"Where did it run?" asked Miao Kui.

Gold Tiger pointed to the cliff's edge, "That the trap it set for us. We can't chase it."

Gold Tiger decided to go down the mountain to avoid running into Director Hu in the morning.

8

Gold Tiger was still asleep fast when someone knocked at the door and awakened him. He rose and opened the door, only to see Director Hu standing at the doorway. The bottoms of his police uniform pants were wet, stained with some black soil and grass.

"What's up?" Gold Tiger, whose heart skipped a beat, wondered if Director Hu's targeted monitoring camera had captured him going to the mountains last night.

"You're hiding things from me," said Director Hu, his light brown eyes exceptionally piercing, as if throwing out a pair of sharp daggers.

"I'm not the target of your monitoring system, so I don't need to report everything to you, do I?" He loathed Director Hu's tone and thought he was harassing the people under his jurisdiction by knocking at his door so early in the morning.

"What's happened to Red Mastiff? Why did you lie to me?" Director Hu showed a picture on his cellphone. It's Red Mastiff's burial ground, and its mound was still grassless. *Director Hu has found Red Mastiff's body.* He admired the light-brown-eyed police officer secretly. *How did he find such a small mound in such a big forest? And did he dig the grave up and see everything? Red Mastiff isn't a human. It doesn't have to do with the police's motto, "Murder cases must be cracked!"*

Is it necessary for him to be so concerned?

"You shouldn't have been so interested in a dead mastiff," said Gold Tiger coldly. "A dead mastiff doesn't need a permit."

"I'm interested in all the unusual things in my jurisdiction." Director Hu's remark wasn't unpleasant to the ear, either. "I must warn you again. Don't you dare fool me. The day of Sharpshooter is gone forever. You must face it." Director Hu put his phone back in his pocket and continued, "Red Mastiff's neck is broken. You took Red Mastiff to the mountains and ran into a leopard or a black bear, if I guessed right. You didn't have a gun, so you had to let the dog do the job. Then, you had it killed. Am I right?"

"I didn't take Red Mastiff to hunt. Neither did I run into a leopard or a wild boar," tried Gold Tiger to explain away Red Mastiff's death. "It's death is an accident."

"I knew you wouldn't admit. I have the same warning, 'Let's wait and see!'" With that, Director Hu turned and left.

Watching Director Hu walking into the distance at the door, Gold Tiger thought he should have yielded to him during the shooting match because winning someone he shouldn't have haunted him like a nightmare that he could never shake off. Worried that Red Mastiff's grave was in disorder due to the digging, he found a shovel, put on his jacket, and went to the mountains.

Dew dampened his canvas shoes, which squished as he walked. He didn't have any trouble locating that catalpa bungei tree, which had taken root in his heart because of Red Mastiff. Walking up to the tree, he found the grave mound in pretty good shape. Director Hu heaped it back after digging it up. He shoveled some new dirt and added it to the heap. Gold Tiger stood silent before the grave, leaning on the shovel's handle. He felt sorry for Red Mastiff, which died so prematurely. Red Arrow and Red Mastiff, his two favorites, now became permanent sore spots with him. He said to the grave, "Now that I've found the murderer, I'll never let this cunning beast off. I'll hang it from this catalpa bungee tree to pay homage to you!"

He came to see Miao Kui. He was here to talk with him about the next step, and the talk happened in Miao Kui's tearoom. A baby constantly cried from next door. Gold Tiger knew it was Ji'ao. Each of its crying fits would cause Miao Kui's brows to twitch. Apparently, he loved and cared about his son profoundly.

They couldn't use chickens as baits anymore. The lynx would never be fooled a second time when he saw through their trick. Gold Tiger believed that lynxes were smarter than domestic cats. It's said that they can remember each incident of being hurt or frightened. So, what else could they use? Gold Tiger thought of lambs.

"As a Chinese saying goes, 'Spare your child, and you can't catch a wolf,'" [7] muttered Gold Tiger with clenched teeth. "A lamb would be a lynx's top delicacy. A nursing mother lynx can't resist the temptation of

---

[7] The original proverb was "You can't catch a wolf if you grudge your shoes." Indeed, you have to travel a lot to find the game animal. However, in Shanxi, where the proverb originated, the local dialect "shoes" sounds similar to "haizi," which means "child" in Mandarin Chinese. Hence, the proverb with "child" replacing "shoes" has been erroneously passed on till today. Cruel as it sounds, the current version carries a more resolute or desperate tone.

a lamb."

"A bait may be important, but what shall we do if it doesn't bite it? I think we should use a firearm." Miao Kui rose, opened his iron cabin, and took out a shotgun wrapped in newspapers. "It's made in Austria, a brand-name shotgun."

Gold Tiger unwrapped the newspapers and found it an excellent piece indeed. It's well preserved, with its maple stock as shiny as a mirror.

He gave the gun back to Miao Kui, saying, "I'll continue using the trap. I want to catch the lynx alive. I've promised to Director Hu that I would never use a firearm."

"It's alright so long as we won't let Director Hu know it," said Miao Kui, "If you were caught, I'd take the blame. I'd be fined at the worst."

Gold Tiger shook his head and said, "It isn't a matter of being fined. Once we use a gun, we'll lose in terms of our character. Then, Director Hu's 'Let's wait and see' would see its result. I don't want to give him the chance to exhibit his prowess. But catching a lynx with a trap can prove my prowess. Of course, Director Hu will penalize me for trapping a lynx. But then, my name would change from Sharpshooter to Sharp-trapper. Director Hu's dream of terminating all the hunters in the area will be shattered once and for all. That's because he can't confiscate all the ropes."

"When shall we go to the mountains again?" Miao Kui wished to go that night. Ji'ao's cry seemed to urge him to set off as soon as possible.

"Tomorrow. But I'll go myself; two people would catch more attention." Gold Tiger had made up his mind to go by himself. He told Miao Kui that he and the security guard would drive the herd to the mountains, where he would let the guard take care of the sheep and go to Sifangtai himself.

"I can trap it," said Gold Tiger, "If I failed, I would put the steel-wire lasso over my neck like a noose."

Gold Tiger's remark took Miao Kui aback. He thought that Gold Tiger was betting on his life. He had never heard him swearing like this though he had known him for years. Red Mastiff's death was the motive, alright, but the failures enraged him. Gold Tiger wanted to prove that he was an excellent hunter without using a gun, and by being such, he would shatter Director Hu's dream of being a terminator of hunters in No. 3 Forest Farm. But it was easy said than done!

"Let's not do something stupid, Bro," said Miao Kui with a nervous tone, "If trapping doesn't work, we can think of some other methods."

"Nothing is impossible," declared Gold Tiger, "I'll avenge Red Mastiff while trying to stay alive myself. I'm not a hunter specimen yet."

"You'd have succeeded if you had brought a gun with you last night," Miao Kui mentioned firearms again.

"Don't mention guns again. We must watch out for Director Hu." The mention of guns seemed to become Gold Tiger's taboo. Red Arrow was an unhealable wound in his heart. Since Director Hu told him that all the hunting guns handed in were destroyed, his heart had been bleeding.

"Does Director Hu know our lynx-hunting plan?" Miao Kui always felt uneasy at the mention of Director Hu.

"I don't think so. Besides, where's the plan? Isn't it nothing but a sore point in your mind that you want to remove?"

Miao Kui grinned, "You've got to blame yourself. It would be better if you did not embarrass him during the contest in marksmanship. He's a police station director, after all." Miao Kui thought that Gold Tiger was a bit too defiant. *Director Hu is the boss of the forest farm. Can you still have peace after offending the boss?*

Gold Tiger responded, "It was I who suggested the marksmanship contest. I was the one who accepted his challenge. How would I have gotten by on the forest farm if I hadn't done it?

"I've got an idea," said Miao Kui. "I'd like to invite Director Hu to dinner so that you two can clear the air and forget about your grudges."

"He won't come; the police bans alcohol consumption," responded Gold Tiger.

"Let's give it a try and make it this Saturday," insisted Miao Kui. "I'll go and extend the invitation now."

Unexpectedly, Director Hu agreed to come for dinner at the canteen in Miao Kui's company, and he especially asked that Gold

Tiger eat with him.

When Miao Kui returned and told him about Director Hu's reaction, Gold Tiger saw something ominous in it. *He must be coming prepared. It could turn into a Goose Gate Feast* [8] *in reverse. Since we've already invited him, we have to force ourselves to be good hosts.*

Miao Kui took particular care of the dishes for dinner. There were chicken and fish except for game animals and fowls. Gold Tiger had told him to be careful because Director Hu might come for a fire reconnaissance. "We'd walk into his trap if we fixed something like the 'flying dragon soup' and 'quick-stir-fried pheasants' for him. Miao Kui had moose noses and roe deer meat in his refrigerator. Gold Tiger's premonition made him think twice. He decided not to turn them into parts of the dishes. *Director Hu might try to entrap us, he thought.*

Director Hu came on time and not empty-handed. He carried a five-liter white plastic can, over half of which was filled with the popular moldy bran liquor. He placed the heavy can on the table with a thump and said, "It's seven-year-old heads still from the distiller at Zalantun City, Inner Mongolia, using red sorghum as its raw material. It doesn't go to our heads."

[8] It's a reference to a legendary episode in Chinese history. When two rebel leaders Liu Bang and Xiang Yu vied for taking the First Emperor of Qin's throne, Xiang Yu invited Liu Bang to a banquet at the Goose Gate near the capital of the Qin Dynasty, where his men would ambush and kill his rival Liu. Hence, the "Goose Gate Feast" became a popular topic in Chinese literature and daily life. In this context, Gold Tiger thought that Director Hu might have some bad news for him by readily accepting Miao Kui's dinner invitation and asking him to be present.

Miao Kui had prepared the best brands of baijiu, such as Maotai and Wuliangye Yibin. Director Hu asked him to put them away, saying that if he had drunk spirits of those brands, he would have lost his job as a director of the police station. Miao Kui had to put them back to the liquor cabinet, thinking that Director Hu was pretty generous and down-to-earth.

Gold Tiger was a little embarrassed: he seemed to eat a free meal as Miao Kui had the dishes prepared and Direct Hu brought the liquor. He was quiet and ate and drank slowly, waiting for Direct Hu to break the silence. He knew that people of influence always let others speak first before he could outsmart them. It must be true with Director Hu. Miao Kui knew what Gold Tiger was thinking. He asked Director Hu to drink a few cups and, glancing at Gold Tiger, said, "Brother Gold Tiger mentioned to me several times that he'd like to invite you over. But as you hate bribery, we've never had a chance."

"Gold Tiger has never invited me," Director Hu brushed his flattery aside, "Since he's a respected man in our No. 3 Forest Farm, I would never decline his invitation."

Gold Tiger agreed with Director Hu: he had never asked him to eat dinner with him. He was aware that it was time for him to say something. He stood up and toasted, "Here's to Direct Hu! You do have class: drink the liquor you brought yourself."

"Are you sure you want to drink with me?" asked Director Hu as he gazed at Gold Tiger's winecup. The 20-ml vessel was filled to the brim, with the surface as still as glass. It showed that Gold Tiger's hands were highly steady, a sign of powerful wrists well-trained while shooting his guns. Director Hu had been trained in the military by holding bricks. He could hold a maximum of six. Steady hands and arms are a prerequisite to accurate shooting. A slight quiver of the wrist would cause the bullet to miss a few rings or even the whole target.

"A toast to you," said Gold Tiger as he waited, holding his cup.

Director Hu also rose. He took two bowls over and filled them half full. Then, he held one bowl up and handed the other to Gold Tiger, "Let's drink with bowls."

Gold Tiger measured the liquor in the bowl: at least 150 ml each. Director Hu's toast was hard to decline. Drinking with bowls has been the custom of the descendants of ancient posthouse employees, only that it's out of fashion nowadays. But drinking in such a manner is still seen when old friends celebrate their reunions or locals observe their traditional festivals. Gold Tiger received the bowl and added the content in the small cup to it. He held the bowl with both hands to the level of his lower lip and gulped it down with an even breath. Then, he faced the bottom of the bowl to Director Hu to show he had emptied it. It was also a move of class. If you hold the bowl higher than your head, it's an act of respecting the elders. You keep it lower than your eyebrows to show respect for your peers.

After Gold Tiger drank up his liquor, Director Hu finished his half bowl in the same manner.

After they sat down, Director Hu commented, "Gold Tiger, the way you drink tells me that you are a man who honors his words."

Gold Tiger broke into a smile. The moldy bran liquor Director Hu had brought was intense with a lingering taste. He might be a good drinker, but he was in his fifties anyway. Drinking was fun, but becoming sober again took time. Besides, he seldom drank alcohol in summer. Only before going into the mountains in a snowy winter did he drink half a bowl of moldy bran liquor. After eating a few morsels of the dishes, Director Hu drank a toast in return the way Gold Tiger had toasted him. After consuming two half bowls of the liquor, Gold Tiger's face flushed like the afterglow, whereas Director Hu's was as sallow as a tobacco leaf.

"In fact, part of what I did had to do with my responsibility. I may have done it too rigidly, but I hope you can understand," said Director Hu with a relaxed expression.

"Face is as vital to a man as the bark is to a tree. It's the hunter's lousy habit to love his face, or honor, too much, said Gold Tiger with the same sincerity.

"Some ideas are like a dynamite fuse. It's better to snuff it out." Director Hu abruptly changed the topic of the conversation and blurted out this seemingly irrelevant remark.

Gold Tiger obviously got his message. He thought for a while and picked up the thread of the conversation, "What you said may make sense, but who won't fire a few firecrackers on New Year's Eve?"

Director Hu responded, "Before the public bulletin was posted, no one cared about what firecrackers you set off. But after that, doing it would get you in trouble."

Fearing that the two might get into a row, Miao Kui hurried to defuse the situation, "Firecrackers are playthings. We aren't children. Let's keep drinking."

Miao Kui poured half a bowl of the liquor for himself and was about to refill the cup for Director Hu when the latter reached out to stop him, "You can't drink. I've seen you drunk and carried home by someone."

Director Hu is sharp, thought Miao Kui. One day, he got drunk after drinking with a customer who had come to the forest farm to purchase merchandise. The owner of the restaurant took him home. Very few people knew the incident, but the fact that he had learned about all the details showed that he had eyes and ears everywhere.

"You can't drink. Gold Tiger has no problem. Those who flush when drinking can drink a lot." Director Hu's remark was a bit provocative.

As a matter of fact, Gold Tiger also had difficulty drinking anymore, but he must take the challenge. Although he might not know how much Director Hu could drink, he believed that Director Hu came today to drink him under the table. No one had gotten him inebriated as the most famous hunter in No. 3 Forest Farm because the posthouse ancestors had bequeathed their descendants the genes of remarkable tolerance for alcohol. He could have drunk quite a while with Director Hu. But he wasn't so sure about the liquor he had brought. He had no confidence in taking the seven-year-old heads still from the distiller at Zalantun City. As his rival had made his challenge explicit, he mustn't shrink from it. Placing two bowls side by side, Gold Tiger gestured for the start of the contest.

Director Hu lifted the plastic can and filled the two bowls up. Then, with a severe look, he said, "Someone from the higher authorities will come to check on our job of curbing poaching in the third quarter of the year. They'll make open and secret investigations. So, I don't want to see something bad happen in my jurisdiction."

"All good hunters know where the limit is," said Gold Tiger, not dodging Director Hu's gaze despite its haughty aggressiveness.

Miao Kui was scared. A bowlful of the spirits weighed over half a kilogram. It would knock either of the two out. He meant to stop them. But seeing them in a cockfighting posture, he was afraid of saying anything. But he groaned inwardly and begged in secret, "Oh, Brother Gold Tiger, could you please raise the white flag? How come you're as stubborn as you were at the shooting contest?"

"I like drinking with a big bowl!" Gold Tiger held up the bowl, his hands still steady.

"I'll drink first as a gesture of showing respect." Director Hu wolfed down his bowlful first.

None showed signs of inebriety. They kept eating, talking, and laughing. Director Hu had no desire to prolong the drinking binge. After finishing a streamed bread, he rose and said goodbye. Before departing, he patted Gold Tiger on his shoulder, "Your presence in No. 3 Forest Farm gives my job as the head of a police station its meaning."

"Sorry I may have been disagreeable, but please pardon me." Gold Tiger tried hard to stand straight. *I can't sway. Otherwise, Director Hu would challenge me to drink another half bowl.* He knew that he got the upper hand in the way he acted. In many cases, the best way to stop an opponent from constantly fighting is to keep what you're worth to yourself.

"A man's drinking manners reveals his character." As he stepped to the doorway, Director Hu turned around and stated, "Be a man of integrity!"

9

Gold Tiger decided to put off the lynx-hunting plan. *It doesn't hurt to treat Director Hu with some respect. We can't humiliate him at such a critical juncture when the higher authorities send someone to conduct open and secret investigations.*

Miao Kui said he would do whatever Brother Gold Tiger told him to.

"Director Hu has some sense of brotherhood," said Gold Tiger. "It wasn't easy for him to toast me and say something conciliatory." Gold Tiger considered his words about the open and secret investigation in the third quarter to be conciliatory. He believed that Direct Hu was tipping him off, forewarning him against violating the law when its enforcement was being tightened.

Gold Tiger was fully aware of Director Hu's suspicion of him. The overt and covert CCTV cameras weren't merely decorative. They were entrapping hunters like game animals. If you carried a roe deer or a hazel grouse down the mountains, you'd probably be ambushed by the hidden police officers before you stepped out of the forest. Gold Tiger reckoned that he had never escaped the CCTV cameras every time he went to Sifangtai. That was why Director Hu had been keeping an eye on him. He didn't get him because he hadn't caught him red-handed. After all, prohibiting hunting didn't mean preventing people from going to the mountains, which wasn't against the law. That was the primary reason that he hadn't been in trouble. Gold Tiger's fundamental judgment was that Director Hu was inexorable and took pleasure in capturing people. But those people were all law-breakers.

For three months in a row, Golden Tiger didn't enter the mountains. He devoted himself to sheep herding instead. Miao Kui, of course, grew anxious. Big Brother Gao called him several times, asking when to hunt lynxes. Miao Kui hummed and hawed with what Gold Tiger had told him: *Lynxes shed hair in summer, so their fur isn't good enough. It's better to enter the mountains after the first snow, as the posthouse descendants have been doing habitually.*

Miao Kui was smart enough to know that Gold Tiger had been trying to lower Director Hu's guard and wait for the best chance to take action. He was fully aware that even if Gold Tiger weren't going to do it for that lynx fur hat, he would avenge his Red Mastiff's death. Gold Tiger was a man as good as his words. He had seen him enter the mountain with a shovel and guessed that he was adding dirt to the mound of Red Mastiff's grave, indicating that he hadn't forgotten the lynx. He had also seen him take the stainless-steel collar with double-row spikes from home, sit on the stone stairs at the gate of the sheep pen, put it over his neck a few times, and rub each spike carefully, with his tears streaming down his cheeks. Twice did Miao Kui catch Gold Tiger shed tears alone quietly. He knew that Gold Tiger was crying for Red Arrow and Red Mastiff.

Director Hu came to the company once during the period. He told Gold Tiger a case of poaching that had occurred in No. 4 Forest Farm. A hunter from that farm had hidden a hunting shotgun and illegally broke into the natural reserve, where he poached a red deer and was caught red-handed. "Poaching in the natural reserve is like robbing a bank. He'll be in serious trouble," said Director Hu. "With his additional crime of hiding a weapon, he'll receive a severe sentence." Gold Tiger was aware of the red line: hunting in the natural reserve, akin to a royal garden, is the most foolish thing one can do. Director Hu obviously made an oblique reference to him by telling him about the case. After all, the director didn't trust him and was worried that he might get himself into trouble.

The excited director also shared his work experience with Miao Kui that day. He said what gave him the most incredible pride was the bronze medal for a shooting contest he had won during a military sports meet. This honor was recorded in the army group's history. He asked Miao Kui, "Do you know my greatest success since I started my job on No. 3 Forest Farm?"

Miao Kui responded, "Of course, you've improved the public order and almost eradicated illegal logging."

"Nah," said Director Hu, "My greatest success was that I've changed Gold Tiger from a famous Sharpshooter to a moderate shepherd."

Casting a leer at Director Hu, Gold Tiger chucked secretly and used the pun sarcastically, "A *yang-guan* (shepherd) is also a *guan* (officer). It means Director Hu has promoted me."

The three of them burst into laughter.

Thoughtless statements made in life often take things in the opposite direction. It's like the occurrence of a car accident soon after the driver bragged about his impeccable driving record. One would tumble if one didn't leave enough room under his feet. Two days after Miao Kui complimented Director Hu for keeping the forest farm safe and free from illegal logging, an awful crime happened in No. 3 Forest Farm. Someone illegally logged 11 centenarian Amur cork trees and 19 mature Manchurian ash trees. It was the first significant case after the order was issued to ban logging in the ancient national woodland of No. 3 Forest Farm. It even alarmed the provincial public security department. The thieves transported the logged trees out of No. 3 Forest Farm down the river and sold them to neighboring counties. The higher authorities took the case seriously and ordered that it be cracked within a specific time limit. Under such tremendous pressure, Director Hu was so anxious that he trotted here and there with chapped lips. Gold Tiger said that the 30 timber trees were not embroidery needles. So, it wouldn't be challenging to find their whereabouts as long as people in a given scope were investigated one by one.

It was Light Snow according to 24 solar terms. [9] That day, it happened to snow heavily in the forest farms. The snow in the mountains was knee-deep. Some foraging rabbits were bold enough to look for food in the villagers' courtyards. Looking out at the black-and-white mountains in the distance through the window, Gold Tiger said to himself, "It's time now."

"I've been waiting for this day for so long," said Miao Kui. "Ji'ao smiled at me last night. I saw that as a good omen."

"I'll go myself," said Gold Tiger. "You're a person of position with an enterprise to manage. You can't afford to get yourself in trouble."

Although reluctant, Miao Kui thought that Gold Tiger made sense. Besides, entering the mountains with him wouldn't help him much, but, on the contrary, his presence might increase the chance to expose themselves. However, he was worried that Gold Tiger's steel-wire traps wouldn't work well. Director Hu didn't have the time to watch Gold Tiger while buried in the case. Additionally, Heavens granted this heavy snow, giving them a lifetime chance. Miao Kui was determined to give Gold Tiger a helping hand to fulfill the lynx-hunting plan they had devised for nearly half a year.

Gold Tiger went to the mountains alone. He wore a sheepskin coat inside-out and a raccoon fur hat, the hunting outfits handed down from the hunters' ancestors. It's easy to conceal wearing the sheepskin

---

® The Chinese lunisolar calendar also divides a year into 24 solar terms beginning with Commencement of Spring, each lasting about 15 days, corresponding to the points spaced 15° apart along the ecliptic. Historically, rural China used the system to arrange their agricultural activities mostly. The Light Snow solar term usually falls in late November on the Gregorian calendar.

coat inside-out in the snow, while the raccoon fur hat can help a hunter disguise himself as a raccoon. A little lamp was scared and struggled in Gold Tiger's arms, not knowing where its owner was taking it. Gold Tiger had tided its four limbs and carried it like a baby.

"Don't be scared," said Gold Tiger, gently patting the little lamb on its head, "We'll be back soon."

The destination was undoubtedly Sifangtai. Gold Tiger trusted his intuition.

He went to the catalpa bungee tree first and went up to Red Mastiff's grave covered in the snow. He stood in silent tribute for a while and confidently pledged, "You'll wait and see. I'll get it and take it here."

Snow buried the otherwise uneven surface of the mountain. He tottered along and kept his footfalls gentle. But he was more worried about the CCTV cameras than the concealed bumpy mountainside. He had to keep an eye out for every suspicious object on the crotches of the trees. Some looked like a monitor, but it turned out to be a knot on a tree when he went around and took a closer look. He thus bumped along cautiously. On his way, he saw many pheasants foraging and numerous hazel grouses perched on the tilia tree by the mountain spring. He also found intermittent pawprints of wild boars and roe deer in the snow. The prints were pretty regular and fresh. He was excited to see them because he had missed them for a long time. He could have traced to their owners soon. But he must move on because an experienced hunter must concentrate on his target, the lynx. He told himself, "I should never be distracted!"

It was extremely quiet Sifangtai covered in snow, which heightened the mysterious atmosphere of the old-growth forest. Gold Tiger felt the knife in his boot, the only weapon for defense. It would be helpful in case of an emergency. As all hunters do, he subconsciously looked around at the surroundings. Suddenly, he spotted a CCTV minicam on the crotch of an oak tree. He was alarmed, realizing that Director Hu had long taken notice of Sifangtai. He didn't notice it during his previous trips but found the blind spot and walked up for a close look, only to find the red indicator not flashing. Gold Tiger was convinced that it was not working because the battery was long due for replacement. He felt relieved. As he was pressured to crack the illegal logging case, Director Hu couldn't juggle the obligations of two jobs. He must have overlooked the CCTV camera.

As he turned to leave, he fixed his eyes on a small jagged crag in the distance. It had been inconspicuously hidden behind the foliage in summer. When the leaves had fallen in winter, it was set off by the snow, lying in it like a boar. Knowing that lynxes liked to rest in the crevices or caves, he sneaked up to check. Since there were no pawprints in the snow, he concluded that no lynxes hid beneath the crag. But he took out the collar with two rows of spikes and put it over his neck. Beasts of prey like lynxes and wolves would attack people's necks first, and the collar could provide some protection for his neck. He even imagined that he would fight it with his bare hands if a lynx dashed out. Though uncertain if he could subdue the animal, he thought he would get some pleasure from fighting the lynx unarmed except with the knife. He believed that the beast couldn't be omnipotent. *Killing it with a single shot would deprive me of the fun. But if I could beat the lynx barehanded, I would create a miracle in the forest farms, where I, the famed Sharpshooter, would become a lynx-hunting Wu Song.* [10] *What would Director Hu think then? I'm afraid he would be so frustrated that his light brown eyes would turn blue.* Gold Tiger touched the collar over his neck, feeling the spikes were close to each other and extraordinarily sharp. He made sure that he wouldn't repeat Red Mastiff's tragedy.

He checked all the crags he could find and found nothing suspicious. He sat down on one to take a break, and when he rose again, his pants were caught on something and badly ripped. Frustrated with the rough luck, he stomped his foot on the crag. But its clopping sound surprised him. He bent down to check, only to see a cave beneath it. He lay down on his stomach cautiously and peered into the cave. It was about two meters deep, a step wide, and half a person high. The air-dried feces showed that it was a lynx den. His heart thumped violently, feeling lucky that he found it by chance after looking for it high and low for so long. But after he examined the cave again, he found gnawed bones with old bitemarks. The thickness of the dirt at the cave opening confirmed that it was abandoned, which meant the lynx had relocated

---

[10] It's a reference to the tiger-slaying Wu Song, a hero in *Water Margin* (《水浒传》), one of the classical Chinese novels. Though fictional, his feat of conquering a ferocious tiger with bare hands has made him a household name.

elsewhere.

He stood up and peered at the misty natural reserve in the east, wondering if the lynx had taken its kittens there. He came to the depression where he had laid the trap, beset with doubts and worries. The Ziziphus jujuba bushes appeared pretty thin. The small opening surrounded by the bushes shone with snow, without even the footprints of a rat. He carried the little lamb over and fastened it to where he had fixed the rooster. Then he walked around the bushes to the end of the gully leading to the cliff. These days, he had felt that the gully here was an excellent place to set traps. Although it was only two steps wide and no more than knee-deep, it was here that the lynx had escaped last time.

It was a risky move to set traps on the cliff's edge at the gully's end. For one thing, there was nothing to hide the traps so that they were easy to be seen by the game animals. For the other, it was a dangerous place, where one could fall from the cliff in case of missing one's steps. Besides, it wouldn't be easy to retrieve if the game hung from the cliff. The wolf he had caught in summer was dangling there, and he had had a hard time dragging it up. But he wanted to take this risky move because it was the best location where the lynx would jump up and down.

He laid a hidden trap made of thick nylon cord and covered it with snow. Any living creature would be caught if it passed by and triggered it.

After he finished, he turned around to look at the lamb. He felt somewhat guilty and thought he should have brought something for it to eat. Starved lambs were vulnerable to low temperatures. He went into the woods to pull some grass and spread it beneath the lamb. It bleated a few times and looked at him with a pathetic look. Gold Tiger ran his hand over its head, saying, "Don't be afraid. You'll stay here for just one night."

Night fell early in winter. As soon as dusk came, he knew that something dramatic would happen. He found the old oak tree on which he had spent the night and dug a hole of half a person deep. Lying in it with his sheepskin coat worn inside-out, he waited for the miracle to happen. He felt that he had a seventy or eighty percent chance. He was confident that it was hard for the lynx to hunt in the snow-covered mountain. Besides, it had its litter of kittens to feed, so it wouldn't stay put when it sensed the smell of a lamb. The only thing that worried him was the sudden appearance of a wolf. But then, he felt at ease, knowing that wolves would keep away from where a lone lynx prowled.

It was getting darker, and the snowfield was hazy. The little lamb felt so cold that it kept bleating. Suddenly, Gold Tiger saw a grayish mass appear from the gully. He was taken aback, wondering where it popped up. It confused him. *What if it doesn't run to the cliff's edge with the lamb in its mouth?*

The grayish mass stopped at the Ziziphus jujuba bushes, seemingly observing the lamb. He rubbed his eyes but still couldn't see clearly. He rose quietly. The grayish mass was so vigilant that it seemed to have heard the stir. It suddenly jumped up and was about to turn to run when a "bang" was heard. The grayish mass collapsed to the snow-covered ground. The gunshot gave Gold Tiger a shudder. He looked around and saw Big Brother Gao walking from behind a tree, followed by Miao Kui. Instead of greeting Miao Kui, he dashed to the Ziziphus jujuba bushes. The grayish mass lying on the snow wasn't the lynx. It was a three-legged fox. Shot in the waist, it was twitching with agony.

"Why is it a fox?" asked Big Brother Gao, who came over with his shotgun.

Gold Tiger grabbed the shotgun from Big Brother Gao's hands and asked in a suppressed voice, "Why you? What did you use a gun for? Do you know you'd get yourself into big trouble?"

Big Brother Gao knew Sharpshooter. He explained, "It's not mine."

"Aren't you from No. 4 Forest Farm? Why did you come here? Did Lao Mo send you here?" Gold Tiger didn't expect that Miao Kui would have invited him. He thought Lao Mo had asked him to help Miao Kui.

"Lao Mo?" Big Brother Gao paused a little and said, "He's dead. He died of rabies. He got bitten by a dog while trying to butcher it. But he didn't go and get a jab of rabies vaccine. There was no way to resuscitate him. Miao Kuai asked me for help."

"Lao Mo's dead?" Gold Tiger couldn't believe his ears.

"It's been half a month since his death. He had been miserable, getting crazy when he saw water." Obviously, Big Brother Gao knew Lao Mo pretty well.

Gold Tiger leered at Miao Kui and asked, "Lao Mo had been confused himself. Do you still believe in what he had said?"

Miao Kui was taken by surprise. If Gold Tiger hadn't asked Big Brother Gao, he wouldn't have learned about Lao Mo's death. His cheeks were burning, so much so that the tip of his nose looked like a chilly pepper. His chest heaved heavily. He would never have expected that he was fooled by a fox, which had foiled the lynx-hunting plan he had worked on for nearly half a year. *Where's the lynx? Where is it gone?* To his bewilderment, it was this disabled fox that stole all the chickens.

"The three-legged fox has gained supernatural power!" Gold Tiger said to himself. It turned out that this injured fox had played hide-and-seek with him all along. When everyone says foxes are clever, they tell the truth indeed. Its frequent escapes from the traps proved its intelligence. While convulsing before its death, the fox raised its head toward the east where the cliff was. "As an old saying goes, 'A dying fox points its head to a mound where its den is.' Its cave must be on the cliff." Then, he turned to Big Brother Gao, "Since you broke the taboo, you'd better bury it."

Big Brother Gao asked, "Bury it in the snow?

Gold Tiger nodded. As a hunter, Big Brother Gao knew the rule of the posthouse descendants. Gold Tiger advised with that in regard, "Don't change the orientation of its head."

Miao Kui handed the engineer spade to Big Brother Gao. The latter dug a square hole in the snow, placed the grayish fox in it, and covered it with the snow. He firmed the snow by stamping on it and smoothed it with the spade as if to plaster a wall.

It seemed that the lynx, a resident of Sifangtai, had indeed relocated. It was most likely that it moved to the natural reserve across the gully the day it had taken its kitten back. Gold Tiger rose on his feet and said, "So much for lynx hunting. As Sharpshooter, I had thought I was capable. But who would expect that a three-legged fox fooled me? We hunters are nothing without our tools."

"Don't move!" A loud command sounded behind the three people.

It was Director Hu! Holding the shotgun in his arms, Gold Tiger stood with his eyes closed, stars swimming like snowflakes in front of his vision. Miao Kui and Big Brother Gao were stunned motionless.

Director Hu grabbed the shotgun and slung it over his shoulder. He then went up to Big Brother Gao and patted him on the waist. Ignoring Miao Kui, the director turned to Gold Tiger and confiscated his knife hidden in his boot. Obviously, he had known where it was. Staring at the embarrassed Gold Tiger, he mocked, "You're a Sharpshooter indeed! Pretty accurate!"

Gold Tiger froze momentarily and said with sincerity, "You won. I'm utterly convinced of your ability."

"Winning or losing is another matter. But by committing a crime when law enforcement is being tightened, you've got yourself into big trouble. You know what? I also admire you because you've fooled me. I almost trusted you," said Director Hu with some conceit. "To be frank, I don't want to see you in trouble."

Gold Tiger reached both hands, meaning to let Director Hu cuff him. The latter shook his head, "Forget it. It's too dark, and the ground is too slippery. How can you walk with the cuffs?"

Gold Tiger asked, "How did you trace us? How did you pinpoint us?"

The CCTV system," Director Hu told the truth, "We'll use drones to patrol in the future. You must face it: the day for Sharpshoot is gone forever."

Gold Tiger realized that when Miao Kui and he entered the mountains, they had never escaped Director Hu's CCTV cameras. He kept another eye on him while engaged in the illegal logging case.

"I also know you've laid a trap," said Director Hu, "Believe it or not, I can find it."

With that, Director Hu went to the shallow gully leading to the cliff. At the gully's end was the trap that Gold Tiger had set. Gold Tiger was curious: he had laid it in the blind point of the CCTV camera, and it was drained of power. How did Director Hu discover it?"

He watched Director Hu strode to it. When he passed by the place where the fox was buried, he slipped on the smooth surface of the snow. Thump! The rifle flew out of Director Hu's raised arms into the air and fell onto the snow. Director Hu slipped down the precipice.

"Gosh!" Gold Tiger darted over and looked down while holding a small tree tight. He found Director Hu's right leg caught in the trap, and he was dangling with his head down. He might have bumped his head into something because he was unconscious. He had lost his cotton-padded police cap to the bottom of the cliff.

"Come and help!" He called Miao Kui and Big Brother Gao over. Together, they pulled Director Hu up. Gold Tiger put his raccoon fur hat on Director Hu's head, oozing blood, which appeared dark in the moonlight. Holding Director Hu in his arms, Gold Tiger called him loud while pinching his philtrum, a traditional Chinese treatment to bring people back to consciousness.

After a while, Director Hu slowly opened his eyes. He looked at Gold Tiger and then Miao Kui and Big Brother Gao, mumbling, "You're still in trouble." He then struggled to stand up, but his waist failed him. "I can't walk," said he with pain.

"I'll carry you down the mountain." Gold Tiger crouched down and asked Miao Hui to help Director Hu onto his back. Then he requested Miao Kui to get the little lamb. With the lamb in Miao Kui's arms, the party stumbled down the mountain.

Before they walked far, Director Hu whispered something in Gold Tiger's ear. Director Hu repeated several times before he caught what he said,

"Don't forget the shotgun. It's the evidence."

Lao Teng's Novella *Hunting the Lynx*: The Adherence to Two Kinds of Ideal Personalities

Tang Shengqin and Fang Wei

Hunting the Lynx is a "new addition" to Lao Teng's series of Animal Fiction. Through depicting a battle of wits between protagonists hunter Gold Tiger and public security station director Hu, the story tells the dilemma faced by No. 3 Forest Farm, a community with a long history of hunting—a dilemma about whether to hunt or ban hunting. By delineating the predicament, Lao Teng explores the emotional relationships between people and people and between people and animals. The author uses the conflict between Gold Tiger and Director Hu as an essential way to unfold his story. In the novella, the author highlights the unity of opposites, which exhibits the humanistic spirit of Confucian culture with "benevolence" as the core and pays tribute to the respective beliefs adhered to by the two protagonists with polarized standpoints.

Lao Teng once said he hoped to build a "literary zoo." Therefore, he has made the relationship between nature and people in his *Hunting the Lynx* the focus of his presentation. Lao Teng is a conservative writer with a high sense of responsibility and mission. He has put his reverence for literature to practice in his literary creation. The Confucian connotation, the promotion of humanistic spirit, and the beauty of classical literature formulate the aesthetic principles of his works. An outstanding fiction comprises many elements, such as appealing plots, elegant language, and vivid images. However, Lao Teng's novels and novellas prefer unfolding events amid conflicts so that their characters' personalities will achieve inner harmony in the unity of opposites.

I

Since ancient times, China's standards for ideal personality have varied in different times. In the pre-Qin period, the Confucian culture with "benevolence" as the core believed that the state of perfection was "cultivating the self, managing the family, administering the state, and bringing peace to the nation." The thought later developed into the personality norms of "propriety, righteousness, benevolence, wisdom, and trustworthiness." However, the decline of traditional virtues in recent years makes people wonder where the core that supports the values of modern people is. Under such circumstances, Lao Teng chooses to stick to his responsibilities and beliefs. He believes that human qualities such as honesty, dignity, principle, benevolence, and kindness are more valuable than ever. In his eyes, the ideal personality is the adherence to inner morality and benevolence. And the harmonious relationship between man and nature and between man and man is the perfect paradigm he pursues.

Hunting the Lynx explains the background of regional culture: Although No. 3 Forest Farm enjoys a long history of hunting, the residents have to give it up after the state's newly issued policy. The story begins with gun confiscation and the famous hunter nicknamed

Sharpshooter's reluctant surrender of his rifle under the call of the national policy. Gold Tiger has a grudge against giving up the sacred hunting career as a renowned hunter. His resistance climaxes when Director Hu of the police station vows to become a "terminator of hunters" in No. 3 Forest Farm. On the surface, the conflict between Gold Tiger and Director Hu was intensified by three incidents: the confiscation of Gold Tiger's gun, his refusal to become an auxiliary policeman, and his being fined. However, these conflicts unfold nonviolently. Emphasizing emotional restraint, the author turns the internal undercurrent of the two men's wrestling into a peaceful harmony. Gold Tiger doesn't think the policy of confiscating hunting guns will doom his hunting career. He hopes to hunt without a firearm to maintain his dignity as a "Sharpshooter." Unfortunately, the hunting tradition in No. 3 Forest Farm has gradually declined due to the government's environmental protection policy, and it has become an irreversible trend. Times are changing, and so are people's ideas. Awareness of environmental protection has given rise to related policies, of which Gold Tiger was fully aware. Therefore, he obediently surrenders his rifle despite his sense of loss. He suppresses his dissatisfaction in his heart.

If the gun-confiscating policy is a turning point in Gold Tiger's hunting career, the change in his feelings toward animals is the genuine cause of his decision to give up his gun. The attachment between animals and the harmonious relationship between humans and animals have made Gold Tiger slowly realize that animals also have feelings. Only when his daughter tearfully complains about his cruelty toward animals and witnesses a mother wolf protecting its pups with its own life does Gold Tiger realize how many sins humans have committed by coldly killing the animals. Gold Tiger applies the author's animal concept to practice: Life in nature doesn't come easily, and humans mustn't advance by stepping on the blood of animals. This empathy among humans, animals, and nature advocates the Confucian spirit of "benevolence." All lives are spiritual beings, and only by loving each other can they multiply in an endless succession. Dealing with game animals, Gold Tiger understands their habits thoroughly. Each time, he is impressed by the spirit they manifest. Therefore, Gold Tiger, a born hunter, can answer the government's call not to hunt wild animals indiscriminately. Here, we can see that "the ecological concept first focuses on the relationship between human beings and nature." [1]

In addition to his personality of benevolence and kindness, Gold Tiger also maintains his dignity and adheres to principles. The novella's title is *Hunting the Lynx* instead of *Killing the Lynx*, which shows that it's challenging to distinguish between game animals. "Lynxes are cunning, fierce, and difficult to catch. Killing shows contempt, like an adult beating a child. It's a cinch. When hunting an animal, you treat it as your equal, and you must be courageous and intelligent." From this statement, it follows that the capture of the lynx can kill three birds with one stone: avenging the death of Red Mastiff, curing Ji'ao of his hysteria, and exhibiting his superb hunting skills. If he succeeds, he'll

---

[1] He Shaojun, "The Revelation of Ecological Literature Represented by *A Story in the Clouds* and *The Forest's Silence*," *Research on the Chinese Contemporary Literature*, vol. 3, 2020.

undoubtedly shatter Director Hu's dream of becoming a "terminator of hunters on No. 3 Forest Farm" while maintaining his dignity. At the root of the conflict between Gold Tiger and Director Hu lies the word "dignity." Gold Tiger believes that confiscating his rifle and monitoring him to prevent him from hunting is tantamount to Director Hu's depriving him of his dignity as a hunter.

After surrendering his rifle, Gold Tiger looked back on his hunting experience. In fact, he still supports national policies, which is illustrated by his release of a fox without hesitation. He also embraces Director Hu's philosophy of "no trading, no killing." Although he hopes to beat Director Hu to regain his dignity as a "Sharpshooter," he never crosses the line. Even though Miao Kui has a shotgun at home, Gold Tiger refuses to use it. He's determined to catch the lynx alive. His decision is based on his confidence in his skills and experience. He thinks he'd lose in terms of his character if he would use it. His adherence to his belief also affects his decision. He keeps his promise not to use firearms and wants to catch the lynx barehanded to avenge the death of his Red Mastiff and cure Ji'ao of his hysteria. He may engage Director Hu in a tit-for-tat battle of wits each time he runs into him, but he secretly admires him for his decisions. It's only that Director Hu's constant suspicions and precautions against him have hurt his self-esteem as a "Sharpshooter." So, he uses the battle of wits and courage to prove that he can capture the lynx without a gun as an outstanding hunter so that he can shatter Director Hu's dream of becoming a "terminator of hunters on No. 3 Forest Farm." The endgame proves Gold Tiger's defeat. A shrewd lifetime hunter falls victim to a treacherous fox while the lynx he has laboriously chased for nearly half a year is nowhere to be found. His setback has profound implications: One would go further and further on the path of wrongdoings. Gold Tiger admits his defeat, and the so-called "dignity" he has defended is nothing but failure. Only when one truly knows oneself can one regain one's dignity. As Mr. Yang Hui puts it, "The countryside can undoubtedly provide young people with the opportunity to aspire for their future. There, they can appreciate the essential value of being history subjects, for their destinies are also highly historical." [2] The same is true of Gold Tiger, whose dignity as an individual eventually gives in to the general historical trend.

II

Lao Teng has a deep understanding of the attitudes of government agencies and officials. He has also written *The Latou Posthouse* and *Training the Goshawk*. Lao Teng's works of this genre are intended to objectively describe government officials' character and psychology. In his *Hunting the Lynx*, the portrayal of Hu, a director of a public security police station, and his devotion to his duties show a side of Chinese officials in the new era on a different level. In the national context of reform and new policy enforcement, Director Hu embodies the Confucian spirit of "taking serving the whole country as one's

---

[2] Yang Hui, "The tradition, People's Ethics, and Realism of *Mao Zedong' Talks at the Yan'an Conference on Literature and Art:* Lu Yao's View on Literature," *Research on the Chinese Contemporary Literature*, vol. 1, 2019.

duty" and "being concerned about one's country and people"—a spirit that advocates the entry of society. Cherishing great ideals and a sense of commitment, he carries out the country's policies on environmental protection to the end as a significant part of his responsibilities to the residents of No. 3 Forest Farm. Director Hu is determined to become the "terminator of hunters" on the farm soon after taking his post therein. And he does what he vows to do: confiscating the firearms from the hunters one by one, and his meticulous work attitude wins the forest farm residents' admiration. As an army officer turned civil official, Director Hu retains the temperament and courage of his military tradition. He hears about the nickname Sharpshooter after arriving at the police station on No. 3 Forest Farm. He wants to find out how good the hunter is as a sharpshooter and challenges him to a shooting contest. But the best marksman in the military has lost the match to this amateur, whose real name is Gold Tiger. Moreover, when Director Hu takes the initiative to "win over" Gold Tiger to his side, the latter has rejected him with slighting remarks, which hurt Director Hu's feelings. The grudge between the two has thus begun.

Director Hu has a pet phrase, "Let's wait and see!" It appears in the novella several times. He says it as a warning. A person who concerns greatly about his honor, he also wants to show his "an-eye-for-an-eye" personality by saying so. When Gold Tiger ridicules him, Director Hu says the pet phrase for the first time. He does so to remind Gold Tiger that he won't relent if he catches him doing something illegal. The pet phrase also indicates that Director Hu wants to do his duty well. Everything happening on No. 3 Forest Farm is under his control, and he can notice and brings the best result to any usual occurrence under his jurisdiction. As the police station director, Hu has an absolute sense of responsibility and mission. He uses the pet phrase to deter anyone who cherishes the idea of violating the environmental protection policy. The conflict between the two protagonists unfolds around this pet phrase. An utterance of "We'll wait and see" implies a lot of concealed wrangling between them. The tit-for-tat battle fills their trial attack and counterattack with tension. In the beginning, Director Hu speaks with Gold Tiger in a retaliatory tone after the latter makes him lose face. But after he gradually realizes that Gold Tiger is worthy of the nickname Sharpshooter, Director Hu begins to admire him secretly. His fear of Gold Tiger being a potential lawbreaker also stems from his admiration for the hunter's prowess. Therefore, he says "Wait and see" every time he senses something unusual in Gold Tiger's behavior. With the pet phrase, he hopes that Gold Tiger will abide by the state law and refrain from deliberately violating it when law enforcement is intensified. Making Gold Tiger law-abiding is conducive to halting the poaching trend and shows his intention to keep Gold Tiger from being caught and put in jail. Director Hu's behavior can be described as empathy for his peer hero.

Lao Teng tends to depict his characters as they change. Neither Gold Tiger nor Director Hu "enters the scene stereotyped." Instead, he let them develop in layers as the story unfolds. Gun confiscation exposes the two's conflict at the beginning of the story. But as the reader reads on, he finds out that their conflict is not a simple confrontation between the bad and the good and that their grudge has its cause. Though treating his rifle as the apple of his eye, Gold Tiger still gives it up in response to the call of the state policy, proving that he is a man of his words. It also shows that he hasn't lost his mind as a career hunter. While hunting, he witnesses many animals' attachment to each other, which moves him so much that he's always filled with compassion for them. Aware that prevalent poaching is detrimental to humanity and nature, he insists on not using firearms during hunting despite his eagerness to outshine Director Hu. It also demonstrates his adherence to his personality and dignity. Director Hu is determined to rectify the hunting behavior soon after arriving at No. 3 Forest Farm. Later, the grudge between him and Gold Tiger has caused him to be hard on the latter on any occasion. However, Director Hu is by no means a relentless officer. He has the grit of a soldier and the pride and confidence of a hero. It shows that instead of homogenizing his characters, Lao Teng always presents the beauty of humanity in the unity of opposites.

III

The subject matter of *Hunting the Lynx* is relatively rare. It shows Lao Teng's focus on regional people's livelihood and the local people's state of mind torn by conflicting thoughts arising in modern times. The whole story is more a contradiction between the modernized policy in the development of contemporary society and the traditional humanistic psych of regional people than a tit-for-tat conflict between Gold Tiger and Director Hu. The people on No. 3 Forest Farm have regarded hunting as their primary occupation all along. In the minds of the local hunters, hunting demonstrates their skills and is also the fundamental means of their livelihood. Even an excellent hunter like Gold Tiger has to be a shepherd after guns are confiscated, and hunting is prohibited. The hunting tradition of generations due to the change of times is naturally unacceptable to the hunters for the time being. It has been the reason for Gold Tiger and his fellow hunters' reluctance to hand in their hunting guns when the gun-confiscating policy is first issued. For them, guns are their lives. As Gold Tiger says in the novella, "No trading, no killing," poaching occasionally happens even after guns are confiscated and hunting is prohibited. Therefore, no matter how tough Director Hu is in forbidding hunting, he can't succeed with action until he can bring as many people as possible to the awareness of the harmonious relationship between humans and animals and humans and nature. Gold Tiger, popularly known as Sharpshooter, has changed his view on hunting due to such factors as the hunting prohibiting policy and Director Hu's vigorous enforcement of it. But his change is more credited to his empathy for the animals, which brings out the Confucian spirit of "benevolence." He has realized that humans are not to advance by walking on the blood of wild animals. As living creatures, they should not pay the price of their lives for the selfish interests of human beings. Humanity's respect for animals is a harmonious, beautiful communion of lives. When humans change their contemptuous attitude and begin to view animals on an equal footing, it means they have regained the beautiful human character that has been lost for a long time.

Golden Tiger's change in his attitude toward hunting is also a process in which environmental awareness is slowly being awakened. The relationship between humans and animals shouldn't be a brutal one between the "hunting" and the "hunted." It should be harmonious coexistence, which is a move from opposition to unity. The causal cycle is self-evident. As a negative example serving as a lesson, Lao Mo is on the opposing side of Gold Tiger and Director Hu. Lao Mo was good at treating hysteria, but he used the lynx hat to exorcise evil spirits—a method as superstitious as unfeeling. He was fond of dog meat, and even Red Mastiff was scared of him, and he eventually died of rabies. His lesson makes us think about the current reality. Consumer society has given rise to the gourmet industry. In the era of material abundance, the mentality of novelty and tasting delicacy is running rampant. Unscrupulous businesses encourage poaching and smuggling wild animals and have thus resulted in the near extinction of many creatures. What's worse, they also spread many bacterias and viruses from animals to humans. The 2000 pandemic has taught us a lesson and set us thinking: should humans take great responsibility for nature's revenge against humans? Have we lost our ancestors' benevolent and kind character handed down to us?

Gold Tiger completely identifies himself with Director Hu's philosophy in the second half of the novella. He agrees with him on cracking down on poaching, admires him for his vigilance and sense of responsibility displayed by his various actions to prohibit hunting, and desires to embrace Director Hu's concept of environmental protection. Then, why does Gold Tiger confront Director Hu to the end? He feels wronged and acts in anger. With opposing standpoints, they adhere to different beliefs. The result is that Gold Tiger has been fooled by a fox acting like a lynx, and Director Hu also sees through his seamlessly devised plan. Gold Tiger tries to prove his ability but fails in the end and has to face the reality that his glorious past has become history. The alert and cautious Director Hu thought that everything was under control, but he was still injured in the trap set by Gold Tiger. So, the two finally get even after a long "wait-and-see" period. But in the final analysis, they share the same compassion for animals and the same beautiful moral characters of benevolence and kindness. It's illustrated by the metaphoric scene of Gold Tiger carrying the injured Director Hu down the mountain at the end of the novella.

Hunting the Lynx embodies Lao Teng's yearning for the ideal personality in the context of traditional moral excellence in today's society. It also represents his efforts to rebuild the spirit of the times. The novella unifies opposites logically and epitomizes the ideal state from personality conflict to harmony. The spirit of "benevolence" and the adherence to beliefs that the two protagonists have displayed transcend individuals because they express a particular ideal personality missing in this era.